Janette Kenny

THE TROPHY WIFE

P9-BZH-824

Harlequin®

TORONTO NEW YORK LONDON
AMSTERDAM PARIS SYDNEY HAMBURG
STOCKHOLM ATHENS TOKYO MILAN MADRID
PRAGUE WARSAW BUDAPEST AUCKLAND

Recycling programs
for this product may
not exist in your area.

ISBN-13: 978-0-373-13030-6

THE TROPHY WIFE

Originally published in the U.K. as THE ILLEGITIMATE TYCOON

First North American Publication 2011

Copyright © by Harlequin Books S.A. 2011
Special thanks and acknowledgment are given to Janette Kenny for her contribution to The Notorious Wolfes series.

Printed in U.S.A.

The Notorious Wolfes

A powerful dynasty, where secrets and scandal never sleep!

THE DYNASTY

Eight siblings, blessed with wealth, but denied the
one thing they wanted—a father's love.
A family destroyed by one man's thirst for power.

THE SECRETS

Haunted by their past and driven to succeed, the
Wolfes scattered to the far corners of the globe. But
secrets never sleep and scandal
is starting to stir....

THE POWER

Now, the Wolfe brothers are back, stronger than
ever, but hiding hearts as hard as granite.
It's said that even the blackest of souls can be
healed by the purest of love...
But can the dynasty rise again?

**Each month, Harlequin Presents® is delighted to
bring you an exciting new installment from
The Notorious Wolfes. You won't want to miss out!**

8 volumes to collect and treasure!

Rafael stood at the back of the room watching Leila, wanting to share every moment of his life with her again.

Desperate to share the future with her, as well, to grow old with her, to watch their children grow into adults.

To be content with Leila by his side.

But this past year had changed them both. She had become a different woman. There was a remoteness about her that troubled him. A shadow in her eyes that begged forgiveness. But from what?

His gut twisted at the possibilities. Had he been so driven to be a success, to prove that his eldest brother, Jacob's, money hadn't been wasted on him, that he'd let the one good thing that had happened in his life slip through his fingers? Had he already lost her to her career? To another man?

No, he couldn't believe his Leila would cheat on him. It was simply that she was not ready to give up her career yet, which meant he had to convince her that the dreams they'd woven together before they married were just as strong now. Just as viable.

All about the author...
Janette Kenny

For as long as **JANETTE KENNY** can remember, plots and characters have taken up residence in her head. Her parents, both voracious readers, read her the classics when she was a child. That gave birth to a deep love for literature, and allowed her to travel to exotic locales—those found between the covers of books. Janette's artist mother encouraged her yen to write. As an adolescent, she began creating cartoons featuring her dad as the hero, with plots that focused on the misadventures on their family farm, and she stuffed them in the nightly newspaper for him to find. To her frustration, her sketches paled in comparison with her captions.

Though she dabbled with articles, she didn't fully embrace her dream to write novels until years later, when she was a busy cosmetologist making a name for herself in her own salon. That was when she decided to write the type of stories she'd been reading—romances.

Once the writing bug bit, an incurable passion consumed her to create stories and people them. Still, it was seven more years and that many novels before she saw her first historical romance published. Now that she's also writing contemporary romances for Harlequin, she finally knows that a full-time career in writing is closer to reality.

Janette shares her home and free time with a chow-shepherd mix pup she rescued from the pound, who aspires to be a lapdog. She invites you to visit her website www.jankenny.com. She loves to hear from readers—email her at janette@jankenny.com.

Books by Janette Kenny

Harlequin Presents®

Other titles by this author available in eBook

CHAPTER ONE

THE crush of beautiful people in this small town on the French Riviera was a treat for the senses, but only one beauty captured Rafael da Souza's attention. She always had from the first moment he had met her in London.

His desire for her had never waned during the five years they'd been married. Nothing would ever change that.

He knew the exact moment strikingly beautiful supermodel Leila Santiago walked into a room, even if he was already prepared. And he was certainly ready for this reunion, body and soul!

Even before they had married, they'd mutually agreed to wait before starting their family. It had been important to both of them that they focus on their careers first. That they enjoyed life and especially each other.

And they had.

Well, almost…

Rafael's brow pulled as he looked back on what was now the fifth year of their marriage. He could count the times he'd been with Leila over this past year on one hand. Her career and his had taken quantum leaps, bigger than either of them could have imagined, but such success came at a terrible price for it had pulled them both in different directions.

Leila had been involved on two whirlwind global tours,

her beautiful face splashed on glossy magazine covers around the world. Rafael's time had volleyed between being technical adviser on one film and developing a cutting-edge mobile phone device that was light-years ahead of the competition.

He and Leila had only managed to find one fleeting weekend to spend together in Aruba following a photo shoot there. Moments alone, undisturbed by their busy careers, had always been precious between them, and although Rafael had tried to talk to Leila about his desire to start a family, the time had gone by too quickly.

"We'll talk about it at the film festival in France," she'd promised in Aruba as she'd planted hot kisses across the taut planes of his belly. And then she'd taken his mind off family and his dream with bold caresses and long leisurely kisses that he'd been starving for.

They'd ended up in bed, arms and legs entwined. Tongues dueling in carnal love. Bodies thrusting together in the most passionate sex he'd ever had with her.

When he was buried deep in her, clutching her to his heart, he felt whole, and they'd both gotten lost in loving the night away. And then their idyll had been over. Rafael had left with the rising sun after Leila had dropped the bombshell that she wouldn't reschedule an upcoming shoot in order to accompany him to his brother Nathaniel's wedding. He'd been too angry and hurt to do more than offer a clipped, "Fine, I'll see you in France."

Now, he certainly intended to do more than *talk* about starting a family. They would have an entire week together in France. While their days would be busy with promotions and such, their nights would be devoted to each other.

His heart warmed at the thought of having children with Leila, of having a home with her that wasn't empty or flat. He'd never had that in his entire life. His mother had loved him, yes, but she had always held at least two jobs at a time to support them, and she had worked incredibly long hours. He had hardly seen her as a child.

As for a home, their small flat in Wolfestone might have been the place Rafael had been raised, but the memories there were painful, suffocating. Rafael had felt only freedom when he had left its cloying grasp. He had moved to a modern apartment in London and then, when he had married Leila, they had bought a luxurious penthouse in Rio, far away from the darkness of Rafael's past.

But though this was his and Leila's residence, it still lacked that life and energy of a loving family that he had felt missing for so long.

Rafael wanted a real *casa* with land where his children could play and make good memories to last a lifetime. A place they could call home, a place they'd feel safe. *Loved.* Everything his aristocratic father had denied him.

Leila knew how much this meant to him and she had shared his dream of having a family.

And, if they were very lucky, they'd realize that dream soon.

Now, as he saw Leila approach and close the distance separating them, his gaze hungrily licked over her like flames on dry tinder, consuming, scorching. It was always like this, the gripping desire that engulfed him whenever they were reunited.

As for his heart…

His heart warmed with emotions that seemed too huge to imagine. He was afraid to look away, to blink, for fear he'd awaken to discover that what he had with her had just been a fantasy.

She was absolutely gorgeous.

And she was his wife. *His.*

Under the rapid-fire flash of cameras, she strode down

La Croisette with her million-dollar smile in place. He knew she wasn't focused on any one person or thing, that her stunning smile was for her legion of adoring fans.

She knew how to make love to the camera, and the lens loved her. And why wouldn't it?

She was a fantasy brought to life. The woman every man dreamed of making love to, the woman every woman wished she could emulate.

Perfection. *Seductive* perfection.

Her mass of golden hair was caught up in a tumble of messy curls that framed a face that had graced every major magazine since she was thirteen. But that gamine child that had launched her career was gone, replaced by a sensual woman who'd worked hard to make a perfectly toned body seem more desirable than voluptuous curves.

Her crimson dress caressed her upthrust breasts and gentle bow of her hips in the warm salt-tinged breeze. He knew every move she made was carefully orchestrated, right down to the metered strides of her long lithe legs supported by killer stilettos. Strong flawless legs that would wrap around his naked flanks in the throes of passion.

Their March rendezvous had reminded him just how much he'd missed her this past hectic year. How he'd taken for granted the exact feel of her silken skin against his fingers and mouth, her erotic scent that clung to him and held tight, her sultry passion that drove him wild in bed and out.

He caught the slight hesitancy in her eyes before she stopped before him, her palms firm on his chest in a familiar way that had been captured on film a thousand times. A touch that left him trembling inside, remembering all that was good between them. All the passion, the pure joy, the bliss of shutting out the world and lying wrapped in each other's arms.

Her gaze made a slow sweep up to his face, and he felt

his own lips pulling into a smile. His hands settled on her trim waist, firm and clearly possessive. Her soft lips beckoned him and he met her halfway for their customary kiss of greeting, but the moment was gone before he could savor it.

Her scent stayed with him though, a provocative perfume that teased the senses. That promised much more. This would be the new fragrance she was here to promote in conjunction with the release of the film of the same name, *Bare Souls*.

That certainly did not describe them!

For as close as they were with each other's bodies, they had both kept their own demons securely locked away since the day they'd met. He'd never told her how being William Wolfe's unwanted bastard had scarred him. She'd never divulged everything pertaining to the near disastrous bout of anorexia she'd suffered at a young age. But he suspected she was still haunted by that episode in her life, and he wondered now if she'd truly fully recovered from the disease.

Those big hazel eyes that had captured the heart of the world at thirteen locked on his and his concerns fled. For a heartbeat it was difficult to breathe. Impossible to think.

Then in a blink the look was gone, replaced with the seductive glint of a woman. The look that had men around the globe drooling after her.

He certainly was not immune! His body responded to the carnal energy arcing between them, and he reached out and cupped her jaw, a simple caress that drew whispers from the crowds.

But it was as if everyone else on the planet faded away until it was just them.

This reaction to each other, this look that they shared and which they had exploited, kept the paparazzi from hounding them with too many questions—specifically about the stability of their marriage this past year.

"How was Nathaniel's wedding?" she asked.

"Everyone asked about you," he said, still hurt that she'd not altered her plans for him. "I called you—"

"I know," she said, her palms shifting against his chest in a small urgent circle, her eyes searching deep into his as if begging him to understand. "I *couldn't* get away."

He nodded, accepting that apology because now wasn't the place to engage in a deeper conversation. But there was a strained note in her voice that had him wondering if she were having difficulties with her career, problems he didn't know about.

If his brothers and sister had thought it odd that the most celebrated model of the decade couldn't demand a day off to attend a family wedding, none of them had mentioned it to him. But then his family was already highly dysfunctional.

They all knew not to expect too much—they were all wary of loving too deeply. And yet love had happened for Rafael. A deep, passionate love that scared him, for he knew that such emotions were fragile. Priceless.

Being with Leila again, knowing she'd be his for an entire week during the film festival, made his skin tighten with anticipation. His heart pounded far harder. Desire. Lust.

Yet, those base emotions were wrapped up in much deeper emotion, like a tight wad that made his blood surge. They had been building toward a far stronger marriage before this past chaotic year.

He fully intended to pick up where they'd left off.

"Our suite is ready," he said.

"Good. I'm eager to sit down someplace quiet for a while."

He cut her a quick look as he took her arm. A sliver of

uncertainty crossed her features again. There was paleness beneath her makeup as well. Had she been ill?

They walked together into the hotel, and he was grateful that velvet ropes kept the fans and paparazzi at bay. He'd never grown comfortable being in the spotlight—spawned from his youth of being pointed out as the Wolfe bastard. Now was no different.

Though he was no longer the subject of ridicule, he still hated the attention that crashed into his private life.

He took Leila's arm and escorted her across the elegant lobby, thankful that they met nobody along the way inclined to ask for an autograph or a quick chat. They were left alone still as they took the elevator to their floor, but Rafael didn't draw a decent breath until he shepherded his wife into their suite and closed off the world behind them. He'd asked for and received a magnificent view of the sea, complete with a private balcony.

"It's breathtaking," Leila noted, pulling free of him and crossing to the bank of windows, and Rafael thought how the view paled in comparison to her beauty. "When did you arrive?"

"Yesterday. I came straight from London."

She faced him then, and backlit with the sun it made her look more fragile and pale. "Were you able to spend much time with your family?"

"I flew in the day of the wedding and left the next morning," he said, then shrugged when her smooth brow pulled into a frown. "Like you, my schedule was incredibly tight."

She nodded at that and looked away. How ironic that he'd kept bits of his past secret from her, yet he disliked it when the tables were turned. He simply saw no sense in divulging how despicable his father had been to him, how he'd suffered emotionally while his siblings had endured that plus physical abuse.

Some things were better left buried. He certainly couldn't see any reason to exhume the dark secrets of his past to his wife.

A good part of his success in business had hinged on his gut feeling to strike deals at opportune moments. This was no different.

"We should coordinate our schedules," he said, smoothly steering the conversation away from his family and their murky past. "My publicist stressed the importance of us showing support for each other and our projects during the festival, though I can't imagine not being there for you."

"Yes, of course. I'll get my mobile."

Was there a quaver of distress in her voice?

He glanced back only to find her riffling through a brand-new designer purse, seeming simply distracted. She was unquestionably the most beautiful woman he'd ever known, but her life was as screwed up as his.

They had been two rising stars who'd collided in a glitter of passion. She had reached the pinnacle of a career that now dictated the way she must live.

Leila was a millionaire in her own right—her name a brand that was copied. Emulated. She had endorsements. Fame. A demanding life far apart from his own.

This past year Rafael had moved from the realm of millionaire to billionaire, and the fast-track world of computer technology meant he always had to stay one step ahead of the competition. He'd honed his rapier-edged instincts in fighting his way to the top of his world, and now he wondered if the changes he saw in Leila had been there all along. If he'd simply been too comfortable with his marriage to recognize his wife wasn't her usual bubbly self.

She certainly seemed more sure of herself than in the past, yet there was a vulnerability about her that hummed about the edge of her success like a nervous hummingbird seeking nectar. There was something wrong that he couldn't quite put his finger on.

They'd both achieved their goals, but at what price to their personal life? Was their marriage still as strong as it once had been?

He'd find out this week that they'd be together; he'd already planned to spend the bulk of his time in his wife's company. He'd missed her more than he could possibly express, for tender words had never been easy for him to grasp, much less admit.

It had always been easier to show her how much he loved her with gifts. Like his latest smartphone.

Rafael ran his thumb over the sleek new mobile that was the cutting edge of technology. This was his baby. The wireless device of the future that was featured in the movie *Bastion 9*, which would premiere here tonight.

But while the phones he'd donated for the elite festival gift bags were silver on black, like the ones that would go on sale tomorrow around the world, this device had a one-of-a-kind liquid magenta shell enhanced with thin black swirls.

Her color.

His mobile was the companion to hers, a reverse of the colors. His and hers phones. A design he'd created as the logo for her own personal line that she'd yet to launch.

"I found it," she said, holding her old mobile up and squinting at the screen.

He held his palm out for it. "It'll take me a moment to exchange the chip into the new one."

Excitement lit her eyes as she crossed to him. "Is that the new device that's all the buzz?"

He nodded.

"I didn't know they came in color."

"They don't, or at least not for a year and even then never with this design."

She reached out and laid her hand on his, stilling him. "Is this design your creation as well?"

"It is," he said, his body surging to life once more by her touch, by the wonder glowing in her eyes.

Her brow furrowed the slightest bit as she studied the intricate swirls. He knew the exact moment she understood the design was much more than lines and curlicues, when she realized this was cursive writing in Portuguese.

"'My only love,'" she read, then pressed two fingers to her lips. "It's perfect."

He'd thought so too. Had believed she was the only woman he'd ever love from the first moment he'd met Leila five years ago.

Leila had been well into making a stunning comeback in the modeling world, but she'd still been a painfully thin waif with soulful eyes.

And it had been obvious she was very much under her dominating mother's control. He'd clashed with the "stage mother" immediately, for at the time he was just a developer in a huge software company in London. A nobody, save the unwanted notoriety of being William Wolfe's bastard, a fact he desperately tried to hide for the shame that it brought on his mother.

Leila Santiago had been the star, hired as the hot model to tout the cutting-edge personal music player he'd developed that recorded and held hundreds of songs.

He'd stood in the shadows of the set watching her, just as he'd watched his siblings play together from afar all those years ago. The longer he'd observed Leila, the more he realized she was dancing to the whims of her domineering mother.

Then as now, Leila's gorgeous eyes had met his. For a

moment he'd seen the pain and uncertainty choking her. Seen the loneliness in her that mirrored his own.

That one look had called to something buried deep inside him. *Bare Souls.*

She, the lost waif in need of a hero, and he, the unwanted boy desperately needing to find the one person who'd make him feel whole. Make him feel worthy.

Everyone on the set had planned to hit the pubs after the shoot and Rafael had looked forward to getting to know Leila better, but her mother had made it clear that Leila needed to work out instead.

Though Leila seemed at her wit's end, she didn't object to her mother's dictates, as if she were used to acquiescing to the woman.

That had been all the incentive he'd needed to approach the alluring model. That and a good dose of arrogant Brazilian pride!

"Join me for a drink?" he'd asked Leila once he'd gotten her alone.

She'd smiled, though it'd been a nervous one. "My mother has already made plans for a trainer to work with me tonight."

He cast her plump mother a scathing glance, for if anyone needed a personal trainer it was her. "Why don't you let her use the workout and you take the night off?"

"With you?"

"Of course."

"I don't even know you," she'd protested, though it'd been a weak one that had encouraged him even more.

He'd introduced himself, and surely made more of his lowly title of software developer than was warranted. But even then he'd had grander dreams. Even then he'd secretly been working on something new and groundbreaking in the computer world.

He'd touched Leila, no more than a caress of her arm. But a jolt of awareness had rocked him to his soul. The sexual attraction jarred him, but not nearly as much as the odd awareness that they were kindred souls.

"Come with me, Leila," he'd said.

She'd cast one look at her mother and bit her lip, but she'd gone with him. For one glorious night and day they'd played like young lovers on holiday.

He'd learned that just one year before she'd collapsed on the runway, and had spent the ensuing long months that followed in a special clinic recovering from the disastrous effects of anorexia. That she'd let her mother take charge of her life, and had yet to build up the confidence again to break free from her.

That he'd been right all along and she was as lonely as he.

That first impulsive date had sparked the whirlwind romance that had rocked the modeling world and set her mother at instant odds against him. He'd fallen under Leila's spell—fallen in love, or as in love as he could be at that strained time in his life.

He'd only known that he'd wanted Leila for more than an affair. He wanted her as his wife. Wanted a family with her.

He proposed marriage, and Leila had eagerly said yes. But she'd made it clear she wasn't ready to be a parent yet.

Neither was he. They'd agreed that family was something they'd start in a few years, after they'd both made their marks. After they'd exhausted the freedom of young love.

He'd known then that one day he'd have it all. A home. A gorgeous wife he loved. And children laughing and playing to chase away the lonely memories of his own childhood.

To give him the family he'd craved, yet had been denied for the most part.

But their wait had stretched from three years into four without Leila and him having a real home. Without Leila being part of his life for one entire year.

No more! They'd both waited too long to see their dreams realized.

He slipped the memory card in Leila's new device and tested it.

"I've taken the liberty to add a few pertinent applications but you'll have to personalize it yourself," he said, and handed her the mobile.

Her fingers brushed his and she jolted, an external reaction to the same bolt of desire that had shot through him earlier, that still simmered deep inside him.

"It looks complicated," she said. "You'll have to show me how to use it."

"We have time to do that later."

Once he'd doused his need to be with her. Once he'd wrestled his control back in place and he could simply enjoy this reunion with her.

He crossed to the tray that had been delivered to their suite and poured an iced coffee laced with *cachaça*. "Would you like a drink?"

"Water with a twist of lime," she said. "I had orange juice at the airport."

He grimaced at the near apology in that confession. She rarely drank anything other than enhanced water which added zero calories. He could count on one hand the times he'd seen her eat a full meal and he'd certainly never seen her binge on anything.

But then he was careful too, moderate. He didn't wish to follow in his own father's alcoholic footsteps.

He turned to offer her the drink and just caught sight of

her rushing into the master bedroom. The closing of the en suite bathroom door echoed softly in the suite.

Not so for the sound of her becoming violently ill. If it were anyone else, he'd pass it off as a malady.

But Leila's troubled past gave him pause.

The unsettling possibility she'd suffered a relapse plagued him as he carried his garment bag and suitcase into the bedroom.

An economy of quick strides carried him into the facility moments after the toilet flushed. She was at the sink rinsing out her mouth, her face paler than before.

"Leila, what's wrong?" he asked.

She shook her head, her eyes bleak. "I've been ill. Some stomach virus that refuses to leave."

"Have you seen a doctor for this?"

"Yes, one who was on staff at the shoot gave me an antibiotic, but he did warn me that if this were a viral infection it would do no good," she said. "I'll be fine."

He gave her a more critical look, wanting to believe her. Yet they'd been apart too much this year, and she'd clearly lost weight.

And though he didn't want to admit it, there was a nervousness about her that hadn't been there before. A withdrawal, almost as if she were hiding something from him.

"Have you tried to lose weight quickly?"

Leila swung around to face Rafael. "No! I'm not a victim of bulimia or anorexia anymore. I simply have a stomach bug. But if you think I'm lying, Rafael, you are more than welcome to ask my agent or my doctor about my health!"

Inferno! He had not expected her to react with such anger, but then he supposed he deserved it for doubting her.

"Forgive me for insinuating you had suffered a relapse," he said, reaching for her, but she turned from him and left the bathroom. Left him standing there feeling like a fool for thinking the worst of her. "I worry, Leila."

She stopped short, shoulders slumping. "I know you do." She brushed a hand through her hair in a show of impatience. "I worry about you as well, but this year—"

Her hand fluttered in the air, and he reached out and snagged it this time. Pulled her close to his heart where she belonged and was glad she didn't resist.

"Things will change now," he said, and gained a shaky nod from her in answer.

This past year had been difficult. Their brief weekend in Aruba sandwiched between her last shoot and his trip to L.A. to consult on the film. This time when they had parted, he'd resented her career more than ever, for it had pulled her from him. Her stellar status had taken precedence over their marriage. Over their plans to start a family.

He'd come close to demanding she take a hiatus from her work. That she embrace her role as his wife again with the same passion as she did her career.

But just realizing that was exactly how his tyrannical father would have acted stopped him.

His marriage to Leila was secure. She loved him and he loved her. They'd just let the outside world infringe too much on their dream.

No more.

Soon he'd plant his seed in her. They'd have their marriage back on track. They'd have a child born of love.

"Dare I ask what brought on your arrogant smile," she said.

His gaze made a slow glide over her face, her breasts, her hips, before returning to her expressive eyes. "I was thinking of how beautiful you'd look pregnant."

CHAPTER TWO

THE thought of being with child pelted Leila like a cold icy rain. She couldn't go through that again, shouldn't attempt it blithely.

Yet like Rafael she longed for a child. A baby to love, to cradle to her bosom. Her and Rafael's child, born of love.

But she'd tried and failed.

Last year Leila had discovered she had been pregnant. But in September, when she had been just twelve weeks along, nature had taken a horribly wrong turn.

Leila had lost her baby. She'd lost a lot of blood. Lost weight. Lost heart over the tragedy.

Her mind ached from the doctor's warning following her miscarriage. Though she was well now, there would always be that chance that due to her anorexia, and the damage it may have wreaked on her body, she could fail to carry a child to term again.

The very last thing Leila wanted was to go through the pain of losing a baby again. She was afraid to try and fail, even though she still wanted to give Rafael the family he craved. Her own arms and heart ached to hold the child she'd lost. Rafael's baby.

But despite her deep yearning for a family, her fear of suffering another miscarriage had grown into paralyzing terror. More so her fear had been given strength when a fellow model, who'd also struggled with anorexia early in her career, had died in childbirth. A woman Leila had admired.

Yet as her friend's body had changed during her pregnancy, the young woman had relapsed into her old destructive habits. Leila had watched as her friend had struggled to regain control of her anorexia, but in the end the disease won, taking her friend's and the baby's lives.

That's when Leila's nightmares had really begun. Now, she wasn't able to think beyond the tragedy her friend had suffered. She had lost confidence that she'd be stronger than the disease.

Her inner turmoil turned into a living breathing hell, for though she still longed to have Rafael's child grow inside her, she couldn't—wouldn't—commit to having a child only to lose it. She suffered this devastation already and it had changed her. But how would Rafael, who wanted a family so desperately, bear it?

Guilt over keeping her terror and her past pregnancy from Rafael roiled in her until her fear became a dragon she didn't know how to slay.

How would he react when he learned she'd kept so much from him?

Not well, she feared.

At the time of her miscarriage he'd been away on some excursion in Brazil, and she knew she couldn't tell him such news over the phone. She could have told him when he returned, in between a break in her hectic schedule, but she'd been so devastated still, so terribly shocked, that she'd been unable to find the words. All too soon too much time had passed. Now?

Leila had no idea how to even begin to tell her husband what had happened! And the timing was once again all wrong.

Leila pushed past his finely honed form and hurried into her bedroom. She simply couldn't deal with it right now, not when her emotions were strained from the flight. Not when she wanted time alone with Rafael first before she voiced the truth that she knew could drive him from her.

She hated that. Hated the distancing between them this past year. But she feared getting close to him again as well. Feared losing control of her body.

And yet that's what her fear was doing now—taking control over her life, her plans, and destroying her dreams.

But how could she risk a repeat of the hell she'd gone through last year? She didn't know, and the uncertainty and fear were eating her alive.

She looked around the room wildly, desperate to regain control of her rioting emotions. Her gaze latched on to the rolling wardrobe clothes rack.

"Is something wrong, *querida*?" Rafael asked, his deep voice freezing her in place for a heartbeat.

Tell him. Blurt it all out!

She ached to turn around and run her hands over his strong muscular chest. Wrap her arms around him and hold him tight. Beg him to forgive her for holding the truth from him.

Leila desperately wanted to hold on to the only man she'd ever loved and savor the moment, for that's all they'd had in a year. Moments.

She'd wanted so much more. She wanted the early days of her marriage back. Wanted the tragedy of her miscarriage forgotten. Wanted to believe that she could bear his child without the mind-numbing fear, that she could be stronger than the disease that had nearly killed her as a teenager. That had killed her friend.

But she couldn't. Not now. Not before the premiere of

the film he'd devoted so much to. Not when the truth could drive an even deeper wedge between them.

"I have to make sure everything I need is here." She moved to the rack, desperately pushing those dark thoughts from her mind.

"Then I will leave you to your unpacking and make a few calls. The premier is at eight, two hours from now."

"I'll have just enough time to get ready."

Without his interference. Without him being so close she could pull him to her, hold him, kiss him.

She'd never intended to keep her miscarriage a secret from him, but her fears had sunk deep roots in her. Her only escape had been her career. It had become her anchor with a new twist. She'd developed a compulsive ritual to oversee her wardrobe, and to coordinate each shoot with the photographer beforehand.

She'd gotten to the point now where she would only work with a handful of noted photographers because they understood her process and brought the best out in her.

But her acclaimed status and demands had come at a price as well, for a few other, less experienced photographers had labeled her a control freak.

She frowned at that fault now, knowing on some level it was true. She tore into the array of garments her agency had provided and nearly an hour passed as she lost herself in the preparations, gaining control of her life and her fear again.

It wasn't easy being at the top of her game. There was no time to sit back on her laurels and savor her position at the top, for there was always a new breed of models eager to knock her off her pedestal.

Time would do that all on its own, of course, as the opportunity for aging models was few and far between. And a model close to thirty was already considered beyond her peak years.

Right now it was crucial that Leila remained focused on her career, and she desperately needed this last campaign to excel. The endowment she would establish off this shoot alone would provide more funding for her clinic for girls battling anorexia and bulimia. So far it had been running on faith and charity. She'd depleted her own funds to shore up their own, but she knew she couldn't keep doing that, knew she needed to do more.

So it was imperative that she let nothing interfere with the networking she must do here at the film festival to secure her clinic. But try as she might she couldn't stop thinking about Rafael.

She couldn't wait to be alone with him, to make love with him, for in his arms the world and its worries faded away.

Leila strode to the closet to hang her personal wardrobe and threw open the doors. And blinked not once but twice. It'd been too long since her things had been next to his. Too long since they'd shared more than a night or two together.

Several masculine suits hung on the rod. Men's fine leather shoes rested on the closet floor in front of a large wheeled case.

A smile curved her lips as she reached out to stroke the woolen sleeve on a charcoal designer suit jacket. When they'd met, he'd barely been able to afford an off-the-rack suit. Now he wore only ones custom-made to fit his long legs, trim hips and broad shoulders.

"Do they meet with your approval?" he asked, his deep rich voice vibrating along her nerves in a delicious hum.

She turned to him with a smile and felt her heart swell with love. With pride, for he'd come from nothing and worked hard to become one of the wealthiest men in the world.

"Yes, I'm impressed by the quality of the cloth and the cut. But then you won me over years ago wearing just faded jeans and a stark-white jersey that hugged your chest—" she paused, striding to him on legs that oddly trembled "—as I long to do now."

A deep growl of pleasure rumbled from his chest as she glided her palms over his honed muscles. "This past year that we've spent apart has nearly killed me."

"Me too," she said, her guilt once more threatening to steal the joy she felt at being in his arms.

Rafael was such a handsome man. So strong inside. So giving to her. So good.

Yet the core of steel within him could be unbendable as well. He was a proud man, slow to trust. And she'd betrayed that bond. Would he be forgiving when she confessed her lie?

"Why the sad look, *querida*?"

She took a breath and debated telling him now. Blurting it out in a rush, then suffering his anger in silence throughout tonight's premiere. No, it would ruin this night for him and he had worked so hard to get to this point in his career.

That smacked of being selfish, and of all her faults, she wasn't that. Nothing could be gained from telling him now.

She'd waited this long to purge her soul. She could wait another day or so until the time was right. Until she'd enjoyed the pleasure of being Rafael's wife and lover without any arguments or hurt feelings between them.

"I was just thinking how nice this would be if we didn't have so many obligations this week," she said.

He shrugged. "Say the word and we'll leave here, go somewhere more private. Just us two."

"So tempting, but you know I can't do that. *We* can't do that."

"When did our careers become more important than our marriage?" he asked.

"It never has been," she protested.

One dark brow arched up. "Hasn't it? In the past year we've only managed to be together once, and that was far too brief."

"I know, but we are both at crucial points in our careers," she said. "To have shirked our responsibilities and commitments would have had adverse effects we might never have recovered from."

Especially for her as a model. Right now it was crucial she kept her name out there. That she stayed on top, for that brought in the big money that enabled her to help others. It gave her purpose and pride to have succeeded so well at something. It gave her control.

But she admitted with a heavy heart that she'd also avoided any kind of close encounter with Rafael after the miscarriage. It had been wrong of her, but she had needed to protect herself. Ah, maybe she was selfish.

What else could explain why she'd done that to the one person she trusted implicitly? Fear, that's what. Losing their baby had been the first tragedy she'd suffered since her recovery from anorexia and it had almost destroyed her.

She had learned a painful lesson. That while she adored Rafael, deep inside was that fear of losing herself if she ever totally put her life in another person's hands again. She had to guard herself closely, for it would be easy to let one compulsion morph into another. For her to slip back to the destructive ways of her teen years.

"I think there is more bothering you than weariness," Rafael said, snapping her attention wholly back to him again.

And my God, but this man knew how to probe one's soul with one long scorching look.

She lifted her gaze just enough to break the magnetic pull that was drawing her closer to him. "I've been on a grueling pace for the past six months. Rest is a luxury I haven't afforded myself."

His dark eyes narrowed, assessing, as if gauging whether to believe her. "Then I insist you enjoy a good night's sleep tonight."

As if she'd be able to do that knowing she had only to reach over to touch him! To slip her arms around that magnificent specimen of masculinity and claim him as her own. That all she had to whisper was *I want you* and they'd both be lost in a passion so deep and so consuming that nothing or no one else would matter.

"You won't get any argument from me," she said, but doubted sleep would come easily for either of them.

Showered, coiffed and makeup carefully applied, Leila slipped into the vibrant blue designer gown that had been provided for tonight's premiere of *Bare Souls*. The skirt was sleek and straight with a side slit to allow ease in walking.

The strapless bodice hugged her middle and flared upward like flower petals to cover her breasts. She had just the right amount of faux tan to complement her natural golden coloring and make her skin glow with this electric shade of blue.

Fiery blue diamond studs sparkled at her ears and a matching pendant with a larger diamond would soon hang from a fine golden chain around her neck. She'd slipped a companion dinner ring on her right hand—all had been birthday gifts from Rafael that had stunned and surprised her.

But she still wore her simple wedding set on her left

hand, and the tiny diamond solitaire and smaller stones in the wedding band winked back at her as if in approval. For years Rafael had insisted on replacing this set with a more lavish one, but she'd told him flat out she didn't want to exchange these for new opulent ones.

These rings meant the world to her for they were the first pieces of jewelry Rafael had given her. These were the rings he'd slipped on her finger—the solitaire when he'd gotten down on one knee and proposed, and the delicate wedding ring when they'd stood before the priest and exchanged their vows.

She hadn't known it was inscribed with *meu coração* until later when her mother had asked to see them up close and she'd reluctantly demurred removing it, the action seeming wrong to her newlywed status. Her pompous mother had scoffed at both the cheap set and the inscription.

But Leila's heart had melted to know he'd done this, for while Rafael was passionate, he wasn't prone to flowery words. She could still count the times he'd told her he loved her.

It was enough, for she believed they'd had a strong marriage based on love. They'd had ordinary dreams of a home and family.

Ah, but neither of their lives had been average. She'd attained great heights with her career again. And with new demands and opportunities came huge rewards.

As for Rafael...

The boy born outside the privilege denied him reached success that trumped her own. That made her achievements pale in comparison.

In short, Rafael was a force to be reckoned with in the business world. More so now.

He'd changed the past year. He now had a ruthless edge

that had only been hinted at before. An edge to him that she wasn't quite sure how to deal with.

Could they regain what they'd once had? Did he even want the same things anymore? Would he still want her when he learned what had happened?

For the first time in her marriage, Leila felt suddenly unsure of her place in Rafael's life. If he didn't want her anymore, if he tossed her aside, she didn't know if she could find the strength to go on. And yet she'd already suffered with worse. Hadn't she?

One sharp rap came at the door. She whirled to face it and froze, still caught up in the old pain and guilt, caught in that very human urge of fight or flight. Before she could move beyond the fear that was crippling her, the door swung open.

Rafael filled the opening, resplendent in black tie, his tux fitting his broad shoulders, muscled torso and long strong legs to perfection. He was, in essence, the embodiment of sexual charm and masculine charisma.

If she'd been startled when she'd stepped from her shower earlier to find him waiting to do the same, she was thunderstruck now. *He could have joined her under the warm spray and she wouldn't have protested!* God knew he had done the same many times before.

So why hadn't he done so this time? Why hadn't he pulled her back into the enclosure and made love with her?

Leila had gripped the counter to steady herself as a wave of hot desire had washed over her. He was simply beautiful. Well toned. Tanned. And aroused.

There'd been no mistaking that part of him.

Yet moments later as he'd stepped from the shower gloriously naked and padded into the bedroom, he'd not spared her a glance. She'd wanted to follow. Wanted to run her hands over his body, wanted to kiss him, taste all of him.

She'd wanted to ease his need and hers as well, for in his arms she felt whole. Safe. Loved.

"God help us both," she'd muttered to herself, and had set to work finishing her hair and makeup. By the time she'd entered the bedroom, he'd been gone.

But now he was back. Tall. Solemn. Sexy as hell.

His dark gaze licked over her, slowly, exacting, a visual caress that left her trembling with need again. Finally, those dark magnetic eyes lifted to hers.

She saw appreciation there and some other emotion that defied explanation. It was a look she'd never seen before, there and gone in a blink. Yet it fed her earlier unease just the same, allowed it to gain a foothold. To grow into another obstacle she didn't need or want.

"We need to leave in five minutes," he said, his voice calm, steady, when her emotions felt as if they were bouncing off the walls.

She swallowed the sudden dryness in her throat and nodded, realizing she still held the blue diamond pendant in her hand. "I'm ready except for my shoes and this stubborn necklace. I can't manage the clasp."

His brows tugged into a disagreeable line for a heartbeat, then quickly smoothed again. "Maybe I can help."

He pushed from the doorway and came toward her, long legs moving with masculine grace. A predator tracking his quarry.

And she certainly felt trapped, for the guilt of withholding the truth from him was ballooning within her.

A shiver rocketed through her as he took the necklace from her and studied the clasp. Yet a smile touched her mouth as she watched him, knowing that rapier-quick mind of his was likely already designing a better clasp for the necklace, one that was user-friendly.

An odd heaviness expanded in her as Rafael fitted the

necklace around her neck and managed the clasp with surprising ease. If only he could do the same for her health issues. But she'd seen a specialist, and the doctor hadn't been able to assure her that she wouldn't suffer another miscarriage.

The blue diamond pendant felt heavy and cold resting between her breasts. Not so for his hands that felt hot and possessive as he briefly skimmed her bare shoulders.

"You look stunning," he said.

"Thank you. So do you," she said, pulling away from him as smoothly as she could so it didn't look as if she was running from him. "You'll clearly attract the eye of every woman here tonight."

He laughed, a rich sound she hadn't heard in far too long. And even that did odd things to her insides.

Good heavens, she would never be able to force a bite down tonight as nervous as she was in his company. Not the way her stomach had been of late.

She slipped her feet into strappy heels, the silver stilettos giving her added height. Now she was nearly eye level with him. On more of an equal footing. And that put her even closer to that devastatingly sensual mouth of his that she longed to kiss.

Damn! Why was she suddenly so obsessed with sex?

"Ready?" she quipped.

"Whenever you are," he said in that same rich tone that hummed along her senses.

She moved to the door. If they didn't get out of this quiet suite, they'd end up in each other's arms. In bed. Locked in passion.

Or battle?

Yes, because she couldn't keep her secret much longer. And she knew he'd be angry when he found out the truth.

She didn't want to fight with Rafael tonight. This was special to him. To them.

"I hope the lines aren't too long," she said, focusing on what was to come instead of Rafael da Souza.

"We'll soon see."

He closed the door behind her and kept pace at her side, not touching her but so close his aura seemed to encircle her. Dwarf her. That was an odd comfort that she grasped on to.

He'd always been her protector. Always had been the one person she could confide in.

And yet she hadn't been able to when it had mattered most!

The fangs of guilt eating at her faded away as they stepped into the limelight. Even in his presence, she still felt like a rare bird in a cage, photographed and ogled endlessly. Being out among the masses was vastly different from a shoot where it was just her and the lens. When she was in control.

She'd never liked this side of her career. This star worship that was as shallow and fake as the artificial minilights twinkling above them.

Before they reached the elevators, she saw the people clustered in the lobby waiting. An old panic began bubbling inside her and she immediately slowed, her gaze searching for another means to avoid this crush.

His hand came up to rest at the small of her back. "Take a breath, *meu amor.*"

She did, then another longer, deeper one. "I don't see anyone I know, at least not personally."

There was no shortage of celebrities waiting in their finery for the elevator. Though she was comfortable strutting her stuff in front of a camera, she hated competing one-on-one with her peers face-to-face!

In her eyes, she always came up lacking. She was still the chubby girl whom her mother had taken in hand and had taught how to rid herself of weight. Who'd learned a dangerous lesson that had nearly taken her life.

"This way," Rafael said, herding her to the last elevator on the left where three men and an elegant woman waited.

She didn't know them, but it was clear by their welcoming expressions that they knew Rafael well. It was the first time that she could recall someone recognizing him before her and the feeling was startling. Almost freeing.

"Good to see you, Rafael," the older of the men said as he extended his hand. "The new phones look fantastic in the gift bags. Before the festival is over, everyone will be clambering for one of them."

Rafael smiled as he shook hands with the man. "I certainly hope so. Please, allow me to introduce my wife, Leila Santiago. Leila, this is the producer of *Bastion 9*."

Introductions were quickly made, and Leila discovered the woman was the producer's wife. The other gentleman was the writer, having just won an award for his original script on a previous movie.

"Our daughter is a true fan of yours," the woman said, surprising Leila. "She dreams of being a model one day and you are the woman she's determined to emulate."

"I wish her much success," Leila said. And none of the heartache.

She fervently hoped that the girl was blessed with a body that remained lithe. That she avoided the pitfalls that had nearly cost Leila her life. That if she did fail, she would be able to find help quickly at a place like her private clinic, where Leila had already given aide to countless other young girls.

The elevator doors opened and they trooped into the

waiting car. Before others could crowd in behind them, she saw Rafael punch the button to close the doors.

She flashed him a grateful smile which he acknowledged with a nod and wink that did odd things to her insides and calmed her as none of her inner talks could. If only he could shut out the rest of the world so easily.

"We have an exciting surprise lined up at the party," the producer said. "You must make an effort to be there at the launch of it."

"Of course," Rafael said before she could say a word. "We wouldn't dream of missing it."

She would. She'd prefer a night alone with her husband. She wanted to unburden her soul. But it would have to wait.

The elevator doors whooshed open and she pushed her way out, eager to get away from strangers. To catch a breath that wasn't laced with the spicy scent that was uniquely Rafael's.

But she got no more than three steps before he was at her side. "Are you all right?"

"You know I dislike small closed spaces," she said.

"As much as I despise the cameras that follow us around." He huffed a breath, and she felt his annoyance vibrate through her in a liquid wave.

Yes, this was her world. She'd gladly guide him through it—as long as he stayed close.

"This red carpet we're about to trod down en route to the Palais du Cinéma is hellish for me too," she admitted.

"You are serious?"

"Very. It's different when it's just me and the camera. I'm in control then. But they—" she nodded at the throng ahead of them "—they are calling the shots now."

"Only if you let them, Leila."

He was right, of course. Still it served to remind her how to get through this crush.

"Just smile. Pretend you see a dear friend just beyond the camera."

"Is that what you do?" he asked.

"Sometimes." But usually she looked for him in the crowd, even though she knew he'd not be there.

He took a breath, then nodded and touched his fingers to her back again. "Let's go, then. The sooner we get through this ordeal, the sooner we can find our seats at the cinema."

And then they'd face the endless swirl of after-premiere parties, the first having already been decided by him. She didn't mind, for one was just like the other. Privacy was a hard-won commodity here.

When they'd reached their plush seats at the cinema, Leila allowed herself to relax. Celebrities, movie moguls and industry professionals all moved to their seats before the lights dimmed.

Later, as the credits rolled, she was stunned at how much Rafael had invested in this film, and not just in the technical support he'd given. As the producer in the elevator had said, every complimentary bag held Rafael's new mobile device. They were as much the talk of the evening as the movie itself with those in the audience activating their phones now.

"I didn't realize they were all operational," she said.

He gave a careless shrug. "I simply provided a month's complimentary service."

The cost of such a move stunned her, for though she knew he'd achieved great wealth in the past year, she'd never dreamed he could afford such extravagance! Did she really know this man next to her at all?

The yacht had been decorated to mimic the set of the movie, a futuristic panorama right down to the uniforms of the waitstaff. The food was lavish. The drinks plentiful.

Stars glittered in an indigo sky and on the decks of the

yacht as well. Leila had adored the nightlife in the early days of their marriage, and would party until dawn with Rafael. But the past few years her enjoyment of the jet-set gaiety had waned.

Even now the best French champagne tasted bitter to her. And the man she'd married seemed a powerful stranger.

He commanded attention. People knew his name. Influential people in all walks of life.

Gone was the carefree young designer who'd created some technological wonder at a time that everyone clambered for something new and groundbreaking. He was a star in his world just as she was in hers.

Only she'd been a comeback queen. It had been grueling to step back in front of the camera after her recovery and she'd been determined to succeed.

Rafael had been her savior then. He'd taken her away from the madness and the pressures of the modeling world. He'd become the barrier that her controlling mother could never break down.

He'd let Leila make her own decisions regarding her career and she had become strong. She owed him everything—including the truth that burned in her soul.

"Rafael da Souza is without a doubt the most handsome man here," a ravishing starlet said, a champagne flute dangling from her jeweled fingers and lust glittering in her blue eyes that were fixed on him.

"I agree," Leila managed to say in a controlled tone, her Brazilian blood bitten with jealousy that this young woman would openly flaunt her desire for Rafael in front of her! "But then, I've always thought he was the most handsome man I've ever met."

"You know him?" she asked, looking at Leila then.

Leila forced a smile, knowing the second when the actress recognized her. "I'm his wife."

And after delivering that statement, Leila walked straight toward her husband. She lifted a flute of champagne off a tray as Rafael turned to talk to a beautiful woman who'd just approached him.

A woman whom he seemed glad to see!

Leila downed the fine wine so fast that her head took a dizzying spin. She refused to rationalize that women threw themselves at Rafael often, for his finely chiseled features and intense dark eyes were too magnetic for any woman to resist, including herself. But he was her husband!

Her sting of jealousy was warranted. Wasn't it?

She wouldn't sit on the sidelines tonight and watch others flirt with him! God forbid if he welcomed their attention, as he seemed to be doing now with this green-eyed beauty at his side.

"There you are," Leila said in an affected purr as she slipped her arms around his muscled one, bringing his startled gaze snapping to hers. "I've missed you."

His brows slammed together, then smoothed one trebling pulse later. "Have you now?"

"I thought perhaps you'd give me a tour of the yacht."

"Later," he said, and flicked an apologetic look at the other woman.

Before Leila could protest, the woman who'd garnered Rafael's attention spoke directly to her. "I've admired your work for years. You make modeling look effortless when I know it is very hard work."

Again she trotted forth her patent smile when she felt anything but pleasant. Her head was still in the clouds from drinking two glasses of champagne on a nearly empty stomach.

"Are you a model?" Leila asked the woman who was as tall as she, enviably lithe and naturally beautiful with a crown of soft brown curls and arresting jade-green eyes.

"Katie is a costume designer," came a deep voice behind her, a voice laced with a distinct English accent. "An excellent one, I may add."

Leila whipped around and stared up at the intruder. The bottom fell out of her queasy stomach as a pair of royal-blue eyes locked on hers.

"Nathaniel," Leila said, noting that the film star was as tall and broad shouldered as Rafael. That their family resemblance was further established with features that were just as finely chiseled.

The look of love Nathaniel and Katie exchanged caught her by surprise. The celebrated star wasn't acting now. This was genuine affection.

"Katie and I were sorry you couldn't make the wedding," Nathaniel said, moving to his wife now and slipping an arm around her shoulders.

"As was I," she replied, her apologetic smile flicking from him to Rafael.

The accusatory glint in her husband's intense eyes scorched through her. He didn't add that she would have known who Katie was if she had accompanied him to his brother's wedding. He didn't have to, for his eyes said it all.

The yacht took a sudden dip and her stomach heaved along with it. Terrified she'd become ill in front of the world, she muttered an apology and fled toward the lower deck and the toilets.

She kept the contents of her queasy stomach, only to find that Rafael had stayed on her heels and was waiting for her to exit.

"Are you ill?" he asked.

She shook her head, for how did one explain one was sick at heart?

"Absolutely not," she said. "I drank too much champagne

on an empty stomach. The movement of the boat made me woozy. Being on the water always does that."

His brow narrowed, as if considering her words. "That is a convenient answer."

"It's the truth. I find these parties cloying," she said. "Maybe I've just been on too hectic of a schedule of late to appreciate the party crowd, but right now I'd kill for some quiet time where I could just relax."

He gave a curt nod. "Then let's leave."

She pressed a hand against the muscled wall of his chest and shivered at the heat and power beneath her palm. "Stay and enjoy your party."

He closed his hand over hers, but his dark gaze gave nothing away of what he felt. "I wouldn't dream of it. If we part company on the first night, the paparazzi will have a field day with speculation."

All for show.

Nobody understood the need for publicity stunts more than she. She'd lend Rafael her support, and he'd do the same for her at the premier of *Bare Souls*. She never doubted he'd be there for her.

But would he once he'd learned what she'd kept from him?

"Besides," he continued, "I've thought of nothing except getting you alone."

"Very well," she said. "Get me out of here."

Rafael kept his thoughts secreted on the short boat ride from the yacht to the dock. He'd said nothing when the boat had picked up speed and Leila had taken his hand in a death grip.

The tremors rocketing through her told him everything he needed to know then. She wasn't fine by any stretch of the imagination. She was putting on a brave front, and if there was one thing he understood, it was how to stand tall in the face of adversity.

His troubled childhood had taught him that bitter lesson!

That's when he'd buried his own pain of being William Wolfe's unwanted bastard into learning the intricacies of computers, discovering what made them work, and what to do to make them work better.

He suspected Leila did the same with her modeling. That was her escape, or perhaps her triumph and celebration, over her bout with anorexia.

His gaze lifted to La Croisette and the cluster of fans, paparazzi and celebrities moving about. The tents crowding the beach were the same, though the lights were more subdued. More intimate.

At one time they'd have enjoyed the nightlife. Now he selfishly wanted Leila to himself. The question remained if she was still eager to be alone with him.

"Would you like to take in the sights before turning in?" he asked, stopping well before the flood of lights spilling from the Palais du Cinéma.

She looked at the active scene they'd soon walk into and shivered. "No. I've no interest in becoming one of the hundreds in the nightclubs."

He released a sigh of relief. "What about the secluded beach? Just us walking, like we used to do."

Music danced on the balmy night air, but he felt the shift in her mood from tense to relieved.

"I'd enjoy that, as long as it takes me away from the spotlight."

He couldn't agree more, and was relieved she felt the same. There was a change in Leila that he'd never seen before, and wasn't quite sure how to deal with. But part of her seemed closed off even to him. Distant. What had happened this past year while they had been embroiled in their careers to put those shadows in her vibrant eyes?

Rafael certainly intended to find out once they were alone. He eased them past the barriers that served to keep the onlookers out and took a trail that wound to a secluded stretch of sand. It wasn't wide and it wasn't pretty, but it was quiet.

"I applaud you for avoiding the paparazzi and the guards," she said, pausing to slip off her heels before they started down the warm sandy coast.

"I was lucky." Just like he'd been all the times he'd sneaked into Wolfe Manor so he could play with his half brothers and sister, defying his father's edict.

He shook off those old painful memories and held on to the good ones. He'd made a solid connection with his siblings over the years, though he didn't keep in touch with all of them. But then his family had remained fractured, with each of his half siblings emotionally or physically scarred by their father.

Rafael had worried that he would not be able to love another person up until the day he'd met Leila. Even during that first year of marriage he'd wondered if what he felt was real. If he'd awaken to discover it had all been a dream.

He glanced down at Leila now, whose features seemed suddenly lighter, freer. He surrendered to his own smile, for there was something about defying the norm that made his own adrenaline surge.

"Feeling better?" he asked, twining his fingers with hers as they struck off down the beach.

"Much. The air is so refreshing."

He made a sound of agreement, though every breath he took drew her sweet scent deeper into his soul. The tension of being the object of so much attention began easing, yet he sensed Leila hadn't let go of it yet.

"I've missed this," she said at last.

"The beach?"

"The peace and quiet with you."

The exact opposite of her lifestyle. Right now at this moment their separate worlds were miles apart. But if they didn't put a stop to this madness they'd lived with for a year, their marriage would surely suffer. Perhaps it already had.

"Why push yourself so hard in your career now?"

"If I don't fight to stay on top of it I could end up on the fringe of this business outside of a year."

Rafael suddenly felt tension seep into his bones. Surely this would happen anyway once they started the family they'd agreed on? Or had that changed?

"It sounds as if you intend to keep working."

"I do," she said without hesitating.

Was she serious?

He wanted a wife and the family he'd long to have. A home. A normal family that he'd always been denied.

He wanted Leila back in his life now, not off somewhere on a shoot dragging their children along. Leaving him behind. Lonely. Forgotten. Rejected.

"And what about children, Leila? I thought we'd agreed that when we started a family, you would be a full-time mother. You'd place our children above everything, and most certainly above your career. Are you telling me now that has changed?"

CHAPTER THREE

RAFAEL held on to his emotions as silence roared between them, obliterating the soothing sounds of the surf washing over the sands and the excited beat of music pulsing in the warm night air.

He'd asked a simple question, one they'd agreed upon before they'd gotten married. The answer should be instant, in keeping with her promise.

"Many mothers work as well as look after their children, Rafael," she said, which sounded like she was building up to an admission that she'd had a change of heart.

He bit off a curse and jammed his hands into his trouser pockets when every cell in his body goaded him to shake sense into his wife. The last thing he needed to do was lose his temper. He had to remain calm. Rational. Or as rational as he could be when his dreams of a family were teetering on the edge.

"Most women with children hold down a job because they have to. You most certainly do not need to work."

"I disagree with you," she fired back. "Many women work because it gives them purpose."

"You think being a mother won't do that?"

He wished he could see her face, but the velvet night swallowed up the details. The tension he felt rocketing through her though was very real, and very telling.

"I can't think of anything on earth that would be as soul-satisfying as having a child," she said at last, her voice breaking a bit with genuine emotion. "But that doesn't mean I couldn't work in moderation. I love my career, Rafael. Through it, I've been able to help other young girls who suffer with eating disorders. I've made a difference in their lives."

He was well aware of the clinic she'd established in Rio and he was proud of all she'd achieved. He was aware, too, that of late she'd suffered a financial setback there. A setback that he could have easily funded for her. But when he'd offered to secure her clinic under his business umbrella in March, she'd thanked him before she'd flatly refused his help.

He'd not brought the subject up again, but now he had to know. "What about your business manager? Doesn't he oversee those issues for you?"

"Yes, but I have final say. Especially with the clinic. It's important to me that I keep a close watch over it," she said.

Leila had as much pride as he. She was also clearly set on having control over her career as well as her charity.

He understood that, for he was the same. But of late he suspected that her drive to make crucial decisions in her life had edged to the extreme. It wasn't just the little things she needed to evaluate. She was micromanaging *everything*.

Their marriage and future family as well?

She couldn't give up her career, and she wouldn't put the management of her charity into anyone else's hands. She insisted she could keep a finger in her work and still be a mother—which she was obviously again trying to put off starting.

He sucked in a breath, then another, but his nerves were still snapping like ribbons in the wind. He knew full well how part-time work could eventually suck up all the hours in a day. He knew, too, how devoted—no, driven—Leila was with her career.

Which made the thought of her being a working mother all the more troubling. A baby could easily be shuffled off while she was busy on a set, cared for by strangers.

Just like his youth? Passed from one neighbor to another while his mother cleaned houses for a meager living. And later, when he was left alone in their small flat when his mother couldn't support them and her various causes with just one job.

Rafael ground his teeth in annoyance, for he'd vowed at an early age that no child of his would endure that type of life. His children would have a home and two parents to come home to every day. They would know they were loved. Wanted. Cherished.

He took her hand and lifted it to his mouth, placing a light kiss on her fingers. A shiver rocketed from her into him, telling him she wasn't immune from him at least.

"Leila, I am tired of us being apart and waiting to start a family," he said. "I want a wife who lives with me again. I want a home and children."

He heard her clear her throat, felt another tremor skitter through her. "God knows I've missed you. But what you are asking me to give up right now is unreasonable."

"No, I am speaking from experience," he reasoned softly. "I lived with a mother who worked all her life, not one but two jobs. I know what it is like to be alone, and I will not put our child through the same."

Before she could answer, a couple's low laughter intruded on them, followed by a barbed comment from a man. He glanced at the sound, noting with irritation that two couples were coming their way, all close to being lost to drink, he'd guess.

"Let's return to our suite," he said, pulling Leila away from the approaching group.

"Gladly."

By the time they'd wended their way through the crowd and into their hotel in brittle silence, Rafael's emotions were stretched to breaking point. At this rate any further conversation about children would likely end in an argument. Yet how could he rest until he knew what had changed Leila's mind?

Dammit, they'd made these plans long ago. Had he simply deluded himself into thinking their marriage and their love was strong?

"It is clear to me that you need to decide what you want," he said, his voice sounding suddenly cold. "A family with me. Or your career."

"Perhaps it is fate's choice to make and not mine."

There was something in her tone that chilled him. Something heart-wrenching in the shadows lurking in her eyes.

Without another word, she slipped into the bedroom. Instead of following, he stood there alone, dreading that there was far more to her prophetic comment than he would like.

Leila jolted awake at the tinny ring of the alarm. She fumbled to turn it off, then sprawled in bed, staring at the ceiling.

The short hours of sleep had left her horribly disoriented. But events of the past day quickly came back in a tumble of bruised memories.

She turned her head and stared at the empty place beside her. The bedclothes were rumpled, the pillow still holding the indentation of his head.

Rafael *had* joined her in bed, but had stayed on his side. He'd deprived her of his comforting arms.

No, that wasn't true. She had been keeping him at an emotional arm's length for too long.

She heaved a sigh and levered herself from the pillow-top mattress. It was certainly the first time they'd shared a bed and not made love. The first time she could recall when they'd gone to bed with harsh words between them.

He'd given her an ultimatum she dreaded to make, for if she gave up her career to start a family, she could lose her baby again. The pressures she had faced in getting to the very top of her career would be nothing compared to that devastation. Yet she knew Rafael would not relent. That he'd push her to be the wife and mother she had once promised and hoped to be.

If only it were that simple.

"Sleep well?" he asked.

She jerked her gaze toward the overstuffed chair by the window. He sprawled in it like a feral cat lazing in the sun.

Her mouth went dry. His broad shoulders and taut ribbed belly were more impressive bare. His skin was tanned. The light sprinkling of black hair on his muscled chest was soft, she knew.

"I rested," she replied, slowly lifting her gaze to his eyes that were wiped clean of the anger that had roiled in him last night. But she didn't kid herself into thinking all was well between them. "When did you come to bed?"

He lifted one broad shoulder. "Close to four."

And with so little sleep he still looked devastatingly handsome. Focused. In control.

She was certainly far from having power over her emotions now. Her eyes felt gritty. Her stomach was a jumble of nerves. And all the grief and guilt she'd suffered this past year seemed to have doubled overnight.

He had to know she'd already tried to be a mother and had failed. That the next try at having a child might not be successful either.

She wet lips that were dry and struggled to find just the right words to tell him about her miscarriage. That she was now terrified to get pregnant, but that her arms still ached to hold her baby close to her bosom. *His* baby.

"Rafael…"

"According to the schedule, you have a shoot in one hour," he said, his gaze now locked on his mobile, brow slightly furrowed.

He was clearly still angry with her and who could blame him. She couldn't very well tell him the truth now and then rush off to get ready for the shoot. He deserved so much more of her time.

"Do you need the bathroom?" she asked, thankful her voice didn't betray the war going on inside her.

"No. Be my guest."

She wasted no time slipping inside the en suite bathroom and by the time she was finished she felt a bit more invigorated.

Yet as she stood in front of the mirror, she could see every new line that had etched her face. She closed her eyes and concentrated on the problem at hand, shoving thoughts of Rafael from her mind. If she excelled at anything it was applying makeup that looked natural, yet took years, and worries, off her face.

If she could only correct the problems with her body just as easily, problems she wouldn't have had if she hadn't developed an eating disorder. But the damage was done, and her guilt ran bone-deep.

Tucking those heartbreaking emotions away, Leila mentally stepped into the role of top model. With her long hair blown dry and silky straight, she slipped on a strapless dress and stepped from the bathroom. To her surprise Rafael had added a crisp white shirt and brown shoes to his ensemble.

He could've been a model.

It wasn't the first time the thought had crossed her mind. He was that put together. That sure of himself.

More sure than she was of herself at this moment and she hated that indecision in her. It had been that inability to make a stand for herself and her career when she had first started modeling that allowed her mother and agent to control her life. To make choices for her that had nearly cost her life. That left her now with damage that could prevent her from ever having a child.

If she could overcome the fear of getting pregnant.

Even then she'd never forget that first life conceived of love. That beautiful surprise that had been taken from her far too soon.

She blinked back sudden tears and checked her purse. Her new mobile rested within, the phone her husband had designed for her, a companion to his own unique one.

It took every ounce of fortitude to tamp her grief and guilt back in its niche. Longer still to remember how to bring up the calendar that would refresh her memory of the location.

She rattled off the address, carefully avoiding meeting Rafael's gaze. "I should be finished by noon."

"Good. We can take lunch afterward."

"That would be perfect. I'll call you when I am free." She slipped her bare feet into an empowering pair of designer slings and moved to the door with determined strides that she hoped wouldn't be interpreted for what they were—a desperate escape from the past that festered inside her.

"No need. I'll be there with you."

That brought her up short and whirling to face him.

"What? Why? You'll be bored to tears watching a shoot—it could go on for hours."

His smile came quickly and rocked the hold she had choked on her emotions. "*Querida*, I will never tire of watching you."

A quiver of excitement skittered through her, but she quickly reminded herself of his deepest desire—to convince her to give up her career and start a family, and she knew she had to be strong.

But as his dark gaze glided over her it made her feel weak. Her skin pebbled, her nipples hardened and ached for his touch, and the most damning was the heat in his eyes that melted her resolve.

Dangerous. He was the most dangerous man she'd ever met. A predator who knew how to stalk his prey—find its vulnerability.

Yet even knowing that, she couldn't find the strength to pull away from him. Moth to flame.

They'd certainly burn together.

He crossed to her, dark eyes intent, challenging her to argue with him. "Surely you have no objections."

She had dozens of them that all danced around her own guilt over lying to the man she loved beyond reason. But there was no point in voicing them right now, not when he was this close. Not when he looked at her with such wicked passion that she was forced to lock her knees to keep from swaying into him. Not when she desperately wanted him. Now. Tonight. And forever.

When the guilt of hurting him was killing her.

"Of course not. The first shoot is in an old château," she said, slipping her model's persona on and stepping from their suite, for when she was "the diva," she was in control. "A limo should be waiting to take me—" she flicked him a smile over her shoulder "—take *us* there."

"It sounds fascinating," he said, closing the door and following her down the hallway.

Tension pulsed in the elevator as the two of them rode it to the lobby. The possessive hand Rafael kept at her back as he guided her to the concierge desk heaped tinder on her guilt. Keeping secrets was a dangerous game she had never wished to play.

She'd tell him about the baby they'd lost after the shoot, when they were alone. She'd bare her soul about her health and hope he understood what had driven her to do what she'd done.

And if he didn't?

Fear crouched in her heart. God help them both then.

When they arrived at the shoot, the producer was waiting for her with a smile that looked strained. Leila suspected Siobhan's patience had been tested by the little man beside her who was the representative of the client—Coltere Fragrance.

It was well known that this client often caused trouble on the set. She only hoped that Siobhan could keep him in line.

That thought had barely crossed her mind before the client snapped, "Who's he?"

"My husband," Leila answered, aware the only way to deal with him was to dare the little man to object. "Is that a problem?"

"Guests are a distraction," the client said.

That was a fact she couldn't dispute. Especially tall, arrogant husbands who commanded attention! But Rafael had been to some of her earlier shoots and she'd not suffered from his presence. Surely now wouldn't be any different? And if it did?

She would take control. She was, after all, a professional. For this little man to assume otherwise was an insult to her.

"I've been in this business long enough to know how to focus," Leila said.

"Of course you do. Now let's be off," Siobhan said, putting an end to the man's rant.

Rafael kept his distance from the overbearing client by pacing the back of the vast hall in the villa. But he'd only retreated here after he'd seen that Leila and her producer had the client in control.

Watching his wife deal with her business made his chest swell with pride. She was nerves of steel draped in silk and poise. It was clear that she oversaw every detail on the set, and was quick to voice her opinion—and will—when necessary.

She commanded respect. And she got it without question. He could understand why she was reluctant to abandon her career, yet he couldn't see how she could do justice to this and motherhood too. *Why couldn't being his wife and mother to his children be enough for her, like she'd once dreamed of?*

Rafael swore under his breath and paced the length of the hall again. Being in this mansion set him on edge, for it brought back memories of Wolfe Manor with its lush gardens and imposing facade.

But unlike his brothers' and sister's childhood home that had fallen into ruin, this villa was in excellent repair, from the ornate Y-shaped staircase that gleamed a rich walnut to the period furnishing that screamed opulence.

But for all its grandeur, he still felt oppressed here. Just like he had all those years ago as he'd stood at the back fence of Wolfe Manor and stared across the gardens at the grand house, where his half siblings had resided.

He'd longed to be invited inside. To play with his half siblings. To fully be a part of his family. But his father had denied him that right. William Wolfe had let it be known that Rafael didn't belong there among his other children.

The stigma of being unwanted burned his soul, even though his eldest brothers had welcomed him into the family fold well before William Wolfe had died. He'd still been the outsider, the one who went back to his squalid home at night. He'd never forged that connection siblings have just by living together, even though they'd all endured hell that their father had heaped on them. But Rafael still felt like the added appendage, there out of Jacob's and Nathaniel's good graces. Accepted, yet still distant.

Sadly, he felt much the same around Leila.

He stood at the back of the room watching her, wanting to share every moment of his life with her again. Desperate to share the future with her as well, to grow old with her, to watch their children grow into adults.

To be content with Leila by his side.

But this past year had changed them both. She had become a different woman. There was a remoteness about her that troubled him. A shadow in her eyes that begged forgiveness. But from what?

His gut twisted at the possibilities. Had he been so driven to be a success, to prove that his eldest brother Jacob's money hadn't been wasted on him, that he'd let the one good thing that had happened in his life slip through his fingers? Had he already lost her to her career? To another man?

No, he couldn't believe his Leila would cheat on him. It was simply that she was not ready to give up her career yet, which meant he had to convince her that the dreams they'd woven together before they married were just as strong now. Just as viable.

With his mind fixed on doing just that, Rafael turned back to the set where the photographer's assistants were busy checking the light. Amid the flurry of movement, Leila strode from the wardrobe tent which was cleverly concealed by an antique dressing screen, and his heart nearly stopped beating as he drank in her beauty.

Two pale gold straps of gathered fabric crossed at the front over her breasts before tying around her slender neck. From her upthrust bosom, the dress fell to midthigh, adding just enough fullness so the fabric moved with her.

And did she ever know how to move!

The low chatter among the crew stopped and he was certain all eyes turned to her. But instead of walking onto the set where the crew waited for her, she came right toward him.

He was certain his heart would pound out of his chest, that his blood would surely burst his veins the way it surged like a swollen river. She smiled as if she hadn't seen him in months and had grieved every second they were apart. It was a look that said she loved him with all her heart. That she ached to pull him into her bed and her body this very second.

She'd always been just as demanding in the bedroom as he. But she'd never fixed him with this "take me" look in public.

Even if he'd been prepared, he doubted he could have stopped his body from responding so quickly. His pulse quickened, his arousal grew swift and painful.

He ached to rip the filmy gold dress from her and make love to her here, deeply, savagely. To leave no doubt that she was his now and forever.

"Four minutes, Miss Santiago," the photographer said, his voice and presence an irritation to Rafael.

"I'm ready when you are," Leila said, but her focus was on Rafael as she stopped before him.

She swept her hands up his chest to his shoulders, sending a tsunami of desire crashing through him. A low growl escaped him, and her eyes gleamed with wicked intent.

Such a vixen! Still his to have. To hold!

Slowly, her hands glided back down, the nails surely shooting sparks as she scored his shirt before her palms settled over the taut planes of his pectorals. "I was nervous about you being here, but now I'm glad you are. You've always been my rock at shoots."

"The only session I've attended in years was in March, *querida*." And that one had sparked a fierce jealousy in him as well as intense longing.

She lifted a hand and scraped a blunt fingernail along his jaw, and like a match to flint, hot flames of desire ignited within him, burning his resolve to ash.

"Yes, but you were always at the other shoots in my mind," she whispered so softly he wondered if he'd heard her right, her eyes now glowing with affection.

"Miss Santiago, may I remind you that we're on a tight schedule here. Time is money," the irritating client snapped.

With another toss of her sleek silken hair, she strode back to the set before the massive fireplace. A multitude of candles burned in the firebox and along the hearth, lending a warm glow to the gray marble.

But it was Leila that he watched. Leila that his blood heated for. Leila that he dreamed of having soon.

The photographer clapped his hands and his staff scampered to do his bidding. "Miss Santiago, if you'd recline on the fainting couch now," he said, and she immediately did as asked.

That was a personal hell for him, for the moment she stretched out on the couch he ached to join her. Her golden dress draped over her demurely, but a fan directed at her kept the hem fluttering like his heart.

The next hour passed in a blur of pictures of Leila stretching out on the couch. Provocative poses. Innocent ones. Beckoning. Assured.

They ran the gamut and Rafael was only sure of one thing. He had never lusted for a woman as he had Leila. Never wanted a woman as much as he did her.

As lovers, there was no comparison. There never would be.

She looked over at him right then, her eyes beckoning, her head back and turned just so, her slender neck cast in light. And then from the shadows came a masculine hand holding a glass perfume stopper.

Rafael's mouth went dry as the tiny glass bulb glided down her throat leaving a thin bead of moisture in its wake. Almost immediately a seductive heady scent filled the air.

But it was the fluid arch of her back and moan that escaped her lips that nearly undid him. Her eyes were closed now in silent ecstasy. What was she thinking?

You are always there in my mind.

Dared he believe her?

CHAPTER FOUR

"INCREDIBLE session," Siobhan said at the wardrobe door.

Leila trotted forth a smile as the assistant helped her out of the gold dress. "I thought so too."

Though the overbearing client had insisted on butting in, the photographer hadn't bowed to the man's demands and Siobhan had quickly hustled the client off the set. Through it all, Leila had kept her calm just by looking over to see that Rafael was still there.

He was on the phone, and she imagined he was involved in his own business. But still he'd come to the shoot and she could get very used to being around him this much again.

"Enjoy your afternoon," Siobhan said, breaking into her thoughts. "The second session today is at five o'clock on the beach, and the swimsuits are wickedly delicious. Just don't overindulge at lunch!"

As if she ever did. "I'll watch it."

Leila left the wardrobe and Rafael stepped forward, his expression pensive. "What would you like to do this afternoon?"

She glanced through the window at the hordes of paparazzi gathered outside the villa and cringed, for they'd surely follow them. "Anything as long as it's someplace quiet where they can't find us."

"And here I was thinking you thrived before the camera."

"Only when I'm on set working," she admitted. "You know that I treasure my privacy."

"As do I." He caught her hand in his, and she shivered at that first jolt of energy that passed from him to her. "Come on. I know just the place to relax."

In moments he'd pulled her out a side door covered by a portico. A uniformed driver stood beside a sleek red sports car.

"*Merci,*" Rafael told the man, who tossed him the key before walking back to a nondescript economy car where another man waited.

"How did you arrange a car so quickly?" she asked as Rafael opened her door.

"I have connections."

A fact she was well aware of.

"Were you so sure that I'd go off with you?" she teased.

His sinfully beautiful mouth pulled into a smile that left her tingling inside. "I can be very persuasive."

As well she knew!

In moments Rafael had whipped through the congested streets toward the harbor. She leaned back in the seat and savored the vista of clear blue sea crowded with all manner of vessels, of the array of umbrellas strung along the beach like a string of colorful gems.

Of being alone with her husband. Maybe when they stopped she could find the words to tell him of their loss. Maybe then he'd understand her fears and the risks involved.

She studied the people crowded on the sandy beach, certain if she looked hard enough she'd catch sight of one of the noted celebrities. But as always Rafael drew her attention back to him, for he was the most fascinating man she'd ever met.

He handled the powerful car just like he did everything

else—with an arrogant ease that she'd always admired. Quiet control. He'd exuded that aura when she had first met him, even though he had acted carefree. Reckless, almost.

Rafael da Souza had been oh so sure he'd succeed in business. And in love.

"You are going to marry me," he'd said that day he'd taken her away from the chaos of her world and off into a whirlwind jaunt into the mountains.

"Why would I do that?" she'd asked, though the idea of being married to him had thrilled her.

"Because you love me and I love you," he'd said with such surety that she'd fallen a bit deeper in love with him then and there. "We belong together, *querida*."

"Don't be too sure of that!" she'd quipped, though inside she'd agreed.

He was her other half. The one person she'd trusted with her life—her future. Her secrets.

She'd known immediately that Rafael was everything she'd dreamed of having in a husband. Determined. Charming. Fun. And oh so sexy.

He was everything she could ever want for in a lover. For the first time in her life she'd felt sexy, a major improvement, for when she looked at herself in a mirror, she saw a woman who was neither pretty nor plain. A woman lacking any remarkable feature. A woman who felt as lost as she often looked on film.

Yet he'd never ordered her about, never forced his will on her. Instead he'd allowed her the right to do what she'd been denied as a child—to play. To make believe.

Two months after meeting him, they married. A very private ceremony in Rio that her mother had hated, for it had robbed that bitter woman of basking in the limelight of a media wedding.

Leila smiled at the memory, clearly remembering Rafael

and herself rushing from the small church in Rio to the waiting car.

Just like now she'd had no idea where Rafael was taking them. But she hadn't cared. She was with the man she adored, and together they were embarking on a lifelong journey together. Together they would make beautiful love and babies.

How naive she'd been not to realize they'd face obstacles along the way. That the damaging effects of the anorexia she'd battled in her youth would threaten to steal her glorious dreams from her.

"You are awfully quiet," he said.

"I was thinking of our wedding day and honeymoon."

He said nothing for the longest time, but she noted his fingers tightened on the steering wheel. Noticed that a muscle along his jaw grew taut.

"I regret I could only give you a poor man's tour," he said, his admission surprising her.

Was he serious? Did he really think that she wanted or needed to live lavishly?

"I certainly don't," she said, and gained a doubting frown from him before he turned his attention back to the winding road. "I reached superstardom at a young age, Rafael, and was under my controlling mother's rule for some time, as you know. I'd had my fill of extravagance by the time I'd turned eighteen."

"That is good to hear, *querida*."

"It's the truth."

She and Rafael had enjoyed a very simple honeymoon. They'd taken an auto tour of Europe, a leisurely journey where they had shunned tourist traps in favor of exploring each other in sensual detail in a staggering assortment of villas, châteaus, apartments and yachts.

What sightseeing they'd done had been just as laid-back.

It had been the first time in her life that she'd totally relaxed. That she'd been someone beside the sought-after model.

Yet when their honeymoon was over, the real world had intruded. Her and Rafael's careers had become more demanding as time wore on.

Now here they were after a horrid year apart, her burdened with guilt and he expecting her to embrace the one thing that terrified her.

He parked in the harbor lot and pulled a small hamper she hadn't seen from behind his seat. "Ready?"

"For a picnic? Of course."

"Good. If we hurry, we can catch the ferry to Île Sainte-Marguerite."

She blinked, her gaze traveling across the sea to the small archipelago. "Isn't that one of the places we stayed on our honeymoon?"

"It is. You asked for peace and quiet, and this was the first place that I thought of."

What a wonderfully romantic surprise! She pressed a hand to her pounding heart, so touched that tears sprang to her eyes.

"It's perfect."

"I am pleased that you like it," he said, and hurried her down the wharf to the waiting ferry.

Fifteen minutes later they set foot on the jeweled island. "Are you up for a hike?"

It was as if history were repeating itself. "Of course."

She slipped her hand in his and let him lead her down to the coastal pathway lined with botanicals. For over an hour they walked quietly along the pathway, admiring the gorgeous scenery and laughing at the songs from the migratory birds clustered in the trees. The aroma of lavender, eucalyptus and an array of exotic flowers perfumed the air, while the peaceful quiet of the island soothed her soul.

Through the occasional breaks in the forest she could glimpse Fort Royal, but though the scenery was spectacular, she had difficulty taking her eyes off Rafael for long. This closeness between them was what she'd so desperately missed. Telling him now would be the right thing to do, the perfect timing, yet she knew that the truth would shatter this wonderful moment.

Right now she simply wanted to enjoy the day with Rafael. To remember the good times they had once shared and not be plagued by the guilt that rested heavy on her. So once again she tucked those errant thoughts away.

They prowled the old jail, and she laughed as he threatened to lock her up and have his way with her.

They walked hand in hand in companionable silence and at that moment she'd never felt closer to him. It was so easy to pretend all was perfect in their lives.

The trail opened onto a secluded cove where the glimmering turquoise sea lapped gently against the shore. "How beautiful."

"Indeed so. This would be the perfect place for our picnic," he said.

When was the last time he'd taken her on a picnic? Years ago, she was sure, for recently they had never had time for each other.

He spread a blanket while she kicked off her slings, the sand warm under her feet. "I wasn't sure what you'd be hungry for so I asked the hotel to arrange a sampling of light fare. They suggested rosé wine, but I remembered you had liked the sparkling French lemonade when we were here."

"It was wonderful," she said, touched at his thoughtfulness.

Not that her memory was less dim. She could clearly remember him on their honeymoon picnic here as well, how his ravenous appetite had made her giggle, how the wind had tossed his thick curly hair until it was an unruly mop.

How they'd lain on the beach and kissed passionately, working themselves into a fever that had sent them rushing back to their hotel.

"It appears we have cold roast chicken and Provençal salad," he proclaimed as he removed the items from the hamper. "And for dessert, fresh fruit tarts and grapes."

To her surprise her stomach actually growled. Her appetite had been nil of late, but today she was ravenous. For food. For Rafael.

"Me thinks the lady is in dire need of sustenance," he joked, and held a piece of savory roasted chicken to her lips.

"Mmm," she said as she ate from his hand, and then curled her tongue around his finger and drew it into her mouth, drawing deeply before nipping the flesh.

His dark eyes smoldered with sensual energy and an erotic growl rumbled from him. "Leila…"

"You taught me everything I know about seduction, Rafael."

One dark eyebrow winged up in sharp rebuke, but the twitch of his lips proved the chastisement was all for show. "Everything, *querida*?"

She laughed, breaking the seductive spell, as she poured lemonade for them into tall glasses while he sprawled on his back, his devastating smile fixed on her. "I might have thought up a few things on my own."

"Experimenting, eh?"

She tried to mimic one of his careless shrugs. "Want to play guinea pig?"

He levered himself up, his lips mere inches from hers. "With you, I am game for anything."

Before she could guess if he was joking or serious, he pressed his lips to hers. Once. Twice. Nothing more than teasing kisses that heated her blood and had her straining toward him for more.

"I'm starving," he said, pulling away from her when she would have preferred kissing him to eating.

But that too soon became an erotic treat for her senses. They sat facing each other and savored their lunch, each pausing from time to time to feed the other.

"I regret that we haven't done this more often over the years," he said as he glided a finger over her brows, along the shell of her ear and down her neck. "Though I don't think I could be the observer at another shoot like this last one."

Her skin pebbled even as her blood heated. "Was it that boring for you?"

He released a rough laugh. "It was agony watching you stretch and reach for your imaginary lover on that couch," he said, his voice dropping to a husky timbre that stroked over her flesh like an erotic caress.

How could he say such a thing when his hand was causing her undue agony? When she'd focused so intently on only him during that shoot that her own body had nearly betrayed her desire?

"I'm sorry you disliked it."

"On the contrary, *querida*. I ached to go to you, to cover you." He pressed a kiss on the side of her neck, then took a teasing nibble, and she couldn't contain her moan of pleasure. "To strip you of that scrap of gold cloth and make love with you."

A mewling sound escaped her lips, eliciting another sultry growl from him. She'd worked hard to emulate that beckoning look. But she hadn't been able to master it until a wise photographer had told her to envision her lover standing in the wings, watching.

When you see him in your mind's eye, make love to the camera.

And so she had.

But that feeling of satisfaction was nothing compared to truly being in Rafael's arms right now.

His eyes had turned a glittering black, searching, questioning. His beautiful mouth was just inches from hers. So close she could almost taste him.

"Meu amor," he said, before his mouth swooped down on hers, hungry, demanding.

She let out a welcoming cry and threaded her arms around his strong neck, powerless to resist him, to deny them both what they so desperately wanted.

He fell back onto the blanket, drawing her down on top of him. He whispered erotic words of love against her lips, her neck, across the heaving swells of her bosom. She gasped, her back bowing into him, her lips straining toward his.

His kiss was demanding more, and she clung to him, burning for his touch, his possession, demanding the same.

Distantly she heard the birds in the trees. Felt the warm sea-tinged breeze sweep over them. Then a foreign sound intruded. Loud. Jarring. Breaking the mood.

"Damn," he said as he pulled his phone from his pocket and glared at the display. But she knew what it was before he spoke. Knew and resented that her career had intruded on their privacy. "Your next session starts in less than an hour. We'd better catch the next ferry or you will be late."

Two hours later Leila was running on pure adrenaline and willpower. The photographer had struggled to find just the right mix of sunlight and breeze to capture his effect and that had cost time. But the monotony of doing the shoot over and over was draining and, despite a liberal coating of sunscreen, Leila's skin felt uncomfortably hot.

Even Rafael looked weary with his dark sunglasses shielding his eyes and his stark-white shirt snapping in the increasing wind. He hadn't said a word the entire time, but his body language bellowed his arrogant vigilance of her with his rigid posture and crossed arms.

That made his presence as unnerving as it was welcome, for while she appreciated his support, she hated that he stood like a guard over her. Just one cross look had some of the crew taking a wide berth of him.

"That's a wrap for today," the photographer finally said. "We've lost the light."

And she was fast losing her stamina.

The wind and sun had left her feeling baked. Her legs trembled and her knees were weak from holding a pose for so long. Her face ached from holding a sultry look.

But once she'd got over the annoyance of having her private time with Rafael ruined, she'd channeled her energy to the job at hand. In truth she did enjoy working with this photographer, for the emotions he could coax from her were always cutting edge.

Right now those feelings came across easily, for her nerves were still humming with the memory of their amorous picnic on Île Sainte-Marguerite.

She longed to return to their suite and finish what they'd started in that secluded cove, even though it wouldn't be long enough. The premiere of *Bare Souls* was tonight, followed by another lavish party by the client on board another yacht.

As the model for that scent, she had to be there. She had to be "on," pretending that all was perfect in her career and her marriage.

"Fabulous shoot, Leila. You are always a pleasure to work with," Siobhan said. "The white bikini you're wearing and accompanying wrap are compliments of the designer."

"Please thank them for me," Leila said.

She accepted the floral cover-up the assistant handed her and quickly donned it. Like most of the clothes given her, she'd donate it to the charity auction she sponsored, with the money going to fund educations for impoverished young girls in Brazil.

"Tomorrow's shoot is in a vineyard near Nice," Siobhan said. "The limo will be waiting for you in the morning."

She managed a nod and mumbled her thanks. If she stayed up late tonight, she'd be dragging in the morning. That was a laugh! She was exhausted now.

Leila wet her dry lips and took a dizzying step toward the cabana, her thoughts spinning as wildly as the lights strung between the tents. The intensity of the sun seemed far more brutal even though the temperatures were on the warm pleasant side now.

Her legs trembled with each step, as if she was moving in slow motion. Not so for Rafael.

He came toward her with surprising speed. "Leila, what's wrong?"

She blinked, but the yellow and black spots continued to dance in front of her eyes. "I don't know."

"Maldição!" Strong arms swept her up and carried her inside the cool confines of the cabana.

She felt him lower her onto the plush cushions, felt the breeze whisper over her body as the punishing glare of the sun was blotted out.

Something cool was pressed to her forehead, her throat, and she moaned her pleasure. She forced open her eyes, blinking rapidly as the blur of colors slowly cleared.

A moment of uncertainty hit her before she remembered what had happened. She'd fainted. She *never* fainted.

To do so was too close to the collapse she'd had as a teenager when her body had refused to continue down the destructive course she'd taken.

Her vision narrowed, focusing on Rafael alone. The stark worry striking bold lines around his eyes and mouth scared her more than her bout of dizziness.

"I'm fine," she said, and made to rise.

He pressed her shoulders back on the chaise. "You are *not* fine, *querida*."

He was right. She was tired. Exhausted. And the festival was just getting under way.

"Excuse me," a stocky man said gruffly as he pushed his way through the crew gathered on the perimeter. "I am Dr. Dubois. How are you feeling?"

"Tired," she said, as he opened a small black case.

"Hmm." He pressed a stethoscope to her chest, listening, his features bland. "Have you been hydrating yourself?"

"Yes," she said. "But this session was longer than most and the sun was brutal."

The doctor gave her a superficial exam. "You should relax and get some more fluids in you. If the dizziness persists, see a doctor immediately. *Oui?*"

"Yes, we will," Rafael said.

"*I* will be fine," she insisted twenty minutes later, more for her benefit than his when they returned to their suite.

"I know you will because I am going to be there to make sure you drink and eat and take care of yourself," he said, looking every inch the arrogant, demanding male.

She hiked her chin up in challenge, refusing to relinquish control of her life, especially when it came to what she ate and drank. "Do you intend to forgo your plans to shadow me?"

"If I must."

Such arrogance!

She kicked off her slings and dropped onto the sofa, hoping she projected an aura of elegant relaxation instead of exhaustion. "I just need to take it easy and I'll be fine."

He looked at her carefully, his early amorous mood vanishing. "You need to relax for a day at least, likely more."

"This isn't a vacation for us," she said.

"What if it were?"

Her head snapped up, her heart skipping a beat on its own. Them on vacation? Together? Like they'd been on the island?

The temptation to lounge and make love and do nothing but enjoy each other like they had in the early days of their marriage was oh so enticing. So terrifying too, for her own love for her husband gave him the upper hand. And Rafael could be so persuasive when he set his mind to it.

Still, she found herself asking, "Where would you want to go on this vacation?"

"Someplace without phones, without crowds, without distractions." His hot gaze slid down her torso and took a slow caressing glide back to meet her eyes. "Someplace were we could be alone to do whatever we wanted whenever the mood struck."

Her breath caught at that, for there had been many times of late when the same idea had seemed so enticing. The escape she needed—yet she didn't kid herself into thinking she'd get a lot of rest if Rafael was with her! Just thinking back to their picnic today proved how they'd likely spend their time.

And wouldn't that be a dream come true, to have him alone without distractions, without plans encroaching on their idyll?

"You'd grow bored without your gadgets," she said, struggling for a light tone.

"Not if you were there with me," he said. "I want my wife back in my life full-time."

The thought was so tempting. To be Rafael's wife and lover as she longed to be. To go to sleep each night in his arms. To wake with him beside her each morning.

Yet he'd made it clear that he wanted more. "You want a child. You want me to give up my career to be a mother."

His gaze caught and held hers. "There was a time when we both dreamed of the day we'd have a family. Were those lies to appease me at the time?"

"No, it's not that at all." She pressed her fingers to her temples, her eyes suddenly burning with tears, her heart aching for what she'd lost. What she could still lose.

Tell him! Trust him to understand!

"My God, I want to have your baby more than anything," she said, her voice cracking with emotion now. "But I'm afraid, Rafael. I'm afraid I'll suffer another miscarriage, or worse."

Rafael froze, his mind taking in her words, processing her admission. Leila had been pregnant before? She'd lost their baby? And what the hell did she mean by worse? What could be worse than losing their baby?

"Leila, you were pregnant?" he asked, gripping her upper arms and jolting when she nearly collapsed against his chest.

He folded her in his arms, absorbing her tremors. She was scaring the hell out of him now, for this wasn't like her. This wasn't the Leila that was always in control.

"I—I didn't kn-know, Rafael," she said between gulping sobs, her tears soaking his shirtfront and burning his skin. "I'm s-so sorry. So sorry."

He pinched his eyes shut and held her, stunned to know

they'd conceived once. That the baby he had wanted so much had been created and lost. No, that *they'd* lost this precious life, for it was clear Leila was just as heartbroken as he.

A thousand questions bombarded him, but he could only force one from his constricted throat. A question that he was sure he knew the answer to, for he hadn't touched her this past year until their quick rendezvous in March.

"When did this happen?" he asked.

She said nothing for the longest time until her sobs gradually eased. Until the tremors that racked her lessened to occasional shivers.

"September," she said.

Eight months ago! He sucked air into his tight lungs, unable to believe she'd kept this from him for so long. That she was only just telling him now.

Anger surged through him, for how could she hide this from him when she knew how much he yearned for a family. "Why didn't you tell me when this happened?"

Her fingers splayed on his chest, but he gained no comfort from her touch, not when his heart was frozen with shock and grief. "You were away in Brazil when I miscarried, busy with your work, and when you returned I was off on location. I didn't see you again until March."

He swore, knowing she hadn't exaggerated. The past year had been a constant whirl of activity for both of them. It had been the turning point in his career just as her own had taken another upswing to launch her into superstardom.

"I wanted to tell you in March," she said, "but so much time had passed by then. And we had so little time together. I didn't want to ruin it by telling you. Please forgive me."

He was mad as hell that this had happened. Furious with himself for being away, that she'd suffered this loss alone.

That she'd grieved in solitude.

He should have been by her side. Holding her hand. Grieving with her. Instead he had been on location with the film company—a remote location deep in the jungle. His phone connection had been virtually nil.

He tipped his head back and let his anger drift from him like smoke from a spent fire, welcoming the pain of grief that quickly threaded inside him to wrap around his heart. Dammit, this hurt like hell.

His hands moved slowly, tenderly, up Leila's spine. He should have been with her, and he'd never forgive himself for being away so long.

She was still burrowed against his chest, but her sobs had lessened and her breathing was somewhat normal. Despite her sorrow, he sensed the steel in her spine, that unbreakable, unbendable will that he so admired. That inner strength that had allowed her to delve back into her work and excel.

"You saw a doctor?" he asked, needing to know why their first attempt at a family had turned out so wrong.

"A specialist," she said, her voice so small he had to bend close to hear her over his thundering heart. "There were more tests. Studies." She shook her head, looking close to tears. "This was my fault, Rafael."

Guilt. He understood it. Felt its fangs sink into him as well. His mind latched on to cold graphic reasons why she would be culpable, then he quickly flung them aside in disgust. Leila would never purposely do anything to put a baby at risk. The doctor wouldn't have looked so stridently for a cause if it had been obvious.

He drew on what little he knew of the chances of conception and miscarriage. "These things are often far from a women's control."

She pushed away from him, shaking her head more vigorously now, looking more miserable than he'd ever seen her look in their marriage. "No, I am to blame. The doctor explained it to me. There is a higher incidence of miscarriage when the mother has a history of anorexia. She said that though I was fully recovered from the disease and have been for years, I am still technically underweight."

The last was said with clear revulsion in her voice. But was she averse to gaining weight because of her history of anorexia? Or was she afraid how added pounds would impact her career?

He'd always accepted that Leila was slighter than the majority of women because of her career. All the top models were lean, without any excess body fat.

He'd come to accept Leila's thinnest as normal. Now a doctor had told her that her low body weight had a bearing on losing their child?

"Help me understand, Leila," he said. "If the risk of this happening again can be lessened when you gain weight and remain healthy, then why are you so gripped with fear?"

She wrung her hands, looking miserable. "I'm afraid, Rafael. I'm afraid I won't be able to cope with the weight I'll gain when pregnant. That I'll relapse. That I'll destroy our baby and myself this time."

"I won't let that happen!" he said, taking her in his arms, relieved she didn't pull away from him this time.

Leila let out a bitter laugh. "That is exactly what I told my friend who went through recovery with me. Who became a model when I did. Who got pregnant a few months before me."

She bunched his shirtfront in her fists and stared up at him with wide tear-filled eyes. "She worried about gaining weight too, but I encouraged her that everything would be fine. That I'd be there with her. That our babies would grow up to be friends. Yet in that month I was recovering from my miscarriage, she relapsed. She lost too much weight too fast and her heart just stopped."

He swallowed hard, feeling her fear and desperation clear to his soul. "I am sorry for your friend, but you are stronger than that, Leila. We are stronger together."

"I know you believe that. And I do want a child. Your child. But now—" Her hand fluttered up and down, much like his hopes for a family were doing. "Please understand. I need to wait."

Wait. They had waited years already to start a family. How many more before she could cope with her fears? Before she'd trust him to protect her?

He wished he knew. "Of course. You need time to heal."

Physically and emotionally, he realized, for Leila looked frail and vulnerable.

"The doctor suggested a year. That I gain weight before I attempt conceiving," she said, a husk of aversion in her voice.

He chose his words carefully. "How do you feel about that?"

"Nervous. But I've gained five kilograms in the past few months." She hugged herself and he caught her frown, a telling gesture that proved she was troubled even by that scant increase. "The change in weight has been hard for me to accept, but I'm trying. I realize I need to feel good at this size before I attempt to gain more."

Meu Deus! This wasn't simply a model concerned over the change in her body. Her statement smacked of a deep-seated fear.

For the first time his mind latched on to the real issue for Leila. The hidden one that she'd been hesitant to voice—to face.

Yes, she had every right to fear suffering another miscarriage. It was likely a concern of many couples, especially when they'd already lost one baby. But he'd never considered that she could suffer a relapse.

It didn't seem feasible to him that a strong woman like Leila would fall victim again to the disease she'd beaten before. But if she couldn't cope with gaining a bit of weight now, what the hell would she do when her belly was swollen with child?

"Perhaps counseling would benefit you again," he said, for when they'd met, she'd told him of the months of therapy she'd taken before she was able to eat normally, though for a model that was still slight portions.

"After my miscarriage, I saw a psychiatrist for weeks," she said, and her tone hinted she was not willing to continue that course of therapy.

Yet she was still blaming herself. But at least she was talking to him, now. That was a start, even though it wasn't what he wanted to hear!

Rafael scrubbed a hand over his mouth and paced the salon.

There were very real and dangerous issues at stake here. He couldn't arrogantly assume that all would be right just because he wanted it to be. Because in the end nothing could guarantee that Leila could have a healthy, happy pregnancy.

Leila… She was his first order of business. He must find a way to help her cope with the guilt and fear that was eating at her. To make her feel at ease with herself, to know that the scant kilograms she had gained only made her womanly curves more beautiful, more desirable to him and to the world.

"There will be no more long separations in our marriage," he said, his mind already figuring out a plan where he could spend the majority of his time with Leila. It was clear she needed him as much, if not more, than he needed her in his life on a daily basis.

That would be especially true once she was with child.

The soft bow of her lips trembled into a smile. "Good. I've missed you so."

That simple admission touched him more than any love profession she could voice. It stripped away their wants and fears and honed in on what they had always had. Each other.

He crossed to her, his hands trembling slightly as he gently cupped her face, his eyes adoring her. "We have a beautiful goal to work toward, *querida*. We have a good future ahead of us. One day we will have a child. A normal family. Trust me."

CHAPTER FIVE

TRUST him? Hadn't he listened to a word she said? Hadn't he understood the risk to her and their unborn child? Her very real fears?

Of course not. It had taken her years to understand that she battled her eating disorder much like an alcoholic avoided strong drink. Because any number of triggers could throw her back into that vicious cycle of anorexia.

She'd stayed strong and healthy because her career demanded it. Because she had an average weight she must maintain to stay on top of her game. She was in total control of every aspect of her life. Being pregnant would be a completely different thing, for she'd have zero control over the changes in her body.

If she failed to cope with her pregnancy—if she was the cause of losing another baby—she'd simply lose her mind.

As for a normal family...

"Would either of us recognize a normal family if we saw one?" she tossed back at him, not bothering to hide the shame of her own troubled childhood this time.

"I know what it isn't," he said, serious as always when the subject of family came up. "Though your family was poor, you had a home, a brother and the love of both parents for much of your childhood."

Leila let out a bitter laugh at that assessment, for it was

far from the truth. "Please, Rafael. You knew my mother. She was not an affectionate woman."

Selfish and demanding, yes. But never loving.

He gave an abbreviated nod, his brow furrowed, likely recalling the rows he'd had with her mother. He'd never been good enough for Leila.

"What of your father? Your brother?" he asked. "You've never spoken much of them, yet they were a big part of your upbringing."

What was there to say about people she hardly knew? About a place that had only existed in her mother's imaginings?

"Home was a shanty in one of the largest *favelas* in Rio. No electricity. No water. After my father died, we were forced to move from our two-room 'home' into a one-room hut."

She glanced at him and took in his stunned expression. She'd shocked him, for like the world he'd believed her mother's lie. That they'd had a small home near the mountains.

Leila heaved a weary sigh and dropped onto the sofa, kicking herself for not unburdening this shame years ago. Her mother had woven a tender, tragic story of being a young widow and single parent that Leila had never disputed, for what was the use?

Unlike her mother, Leila had never courted sympathy from anyone—especially Rafael. But now? She still didn't want his empathy, for she had escaped the fate she'd been born into. But he was asking, and she couldn't continue the lie.

"I don't remember my father, other than he was a stern man who was always away working," she began, her fingers worrying her skirt as she searched her memories and found few good ones to draw on. "As for my brother, he was much older than I was and ignored me for the most part. He worked in the factory with my father, and both died the night it caught fire. After that, my mother sponged off anyone she could for support."

Rafael's brows pulled into a disagreeable V over his patrician nose while his beautifully sculpted lips flattened into a thin hard line. "Why didn't you tell me this years ago?"

She simply stared at him. "What's the use? You never asked, and the truth changes nothing about me. And unless I'm mistaken, you've never divulged everything about your childhood or your family in England."

He jerked his head to the side, his expression hardening, but only for an instant. "You are right. Neither of us had a normal family."

She waited for him to go on. Hoped he would, but he remained silent.

It was just as well. One set of lies revealed in a day was enough for any marriage.

The past was over. Leila had never dwelled on what would have happened to her and her mother if a talent scout hadn't "discovered" the teenaged Leila in Rio. How ironic that her mother had gone to the mall that day to beg for a handout from an aunt who had a soft heart and a job.

Of course that truth had never made the headlines. Instead it was reported that the young beauty had simply been shopping with her mother in the mall.

But that had never mattered to Leila. Modeling had been her chance to have a better life and she'd taken it.

From that day forward Leila had become the breadwinner—the hungry young model who was all the rage, the big-eyed waif to millions and the rising starlet on the fashion scene.

Nobody knew the truth about her past life in Rio. Nobody but her mother.

She pushed aside the old shame and anger and chanced another peek at Rafael. He was far too pensive for her peace of mind.

"You're angry with me," she said.

"Yes," he snapped, and she flinched at the fury in that one word. "Before we married, we vowed we'd never keep secrets from each other. That we'd never set out to deceive each other."

She looked away, blinking back the sudden rush of tears, for there was nothing more she could say in her defense. She *had* lied. She *had* deceived him.

"What's done is done. We reaffirm our vow to be honest with each other always and move forward." Strong masculine fingers cupped her jaw and turned her to face him, face the determined intensity of his eyes boring into her soul. "I am not giving up on our goal or us, *querida*."

She swallowed hard, helpless to stop the tears from slipping from her eyes. He was right. Yet she dreaded to be brutally honest with him about their future as parents.

"Maybe you should."

Silence swirled around them, raising the hairs on her nape, twisting her nerves into knots that pulsed and burned and jumped. "What is *that* supposed to mean?"

"I don't know if I will ever be able to give you the family you want, Rafael! Even if my body can carry a child, I'm not sure my fears will allow me to do it."

"I will not let what happened to your friend happen to you!"

"I know you believe that—"

"Because it is true," he said with so much conviction she almost believed him. Almost. "Our love is strong, Leila. *We're* strong. I will see you have the best doctors. The best care. That you are spoiled and pampered and assured daily how beautiful you are."

Leila released a watery laugh that eased some of the tension gripping him. "I doubt that my agent, clients and photography crew will appreciate me playing the role of diva."

"It doesn't matter what they think, for once you become pregnant you'll give up modeling."

Rafael felt her slender spine stiffen and knew he'd hit a raw nerve. "Whatever gave you that idea?"

Just like that, all the tension that had drained from him went taut as bowstrings. "Isn't it obvious? You are concerned about having a healthy pregnancy. About a relapse. Work would be a great risk."

"One has nothing to do with the other," she said, trying to pull away, but he held tight, refusing to let her run away from him or this issue that stood between them, knowing it would only fester if they left it alone.

"Doesn't it? We are wealthy beyond measure. There is no need for you to be a working mother, to devote your time to a career instead of your family."

Her chin came up. "There is pride, Rafael. You don't want me to work because your mother slaved to provide for you."

"That is some of the reason," he said with a nod.

"Well, I refuse to be like my mother, who never worked a day in her life even when we were close to starving," she said. "She was content to let her husband hold two jobs, and to see her only son follow him to the factory even before he was old enough to do so."

He yanked her flush against him, feeling the thunder of her heart against his chest. Feeling anger course through her at breakneck speed.

"You aren't like her at all," he said. "You could *never* be like her even if you were a full-time mother."

She was shaking her head before he finished. "I will work, Rafael. Maybe not full-time. Maybe only on occasion. But I refuse to give up who I am, what I have worked for."

"I wish you could see yourself as I do, Leila. Then perhaps you wouldn't feel so compelled to prove your worth."

Her chin came up. "Do you really see me, Rafael? Do you truly understand my passions? What drives me? My career funds my clinic and that is very important to me. I won't give it up."

He cut the air with a hand. "You don't have to. I have told you before that I can fund that or any other cause of yours for as long as you wish."

"Yes, but it would be just another appendage of you, instead of mine," she said, fist pressed to her heart.

Frustrated and weary, he threaded his fingers through his hair and paced to the window. On the beach below people laughed and frolicked in the late-afternoon sun. Many couples strolled the edge of the sand hand in hand, just like he and Leila had done earlier today before they had sliced open old wounds and let them bleed freely.

"It's getting late," she said. "I have to get ready." And then she walked slowly into the bedroom.

The soft click of the door echoed in the stillness and reverberated along his nerves. In an hour they'd present themselves to the throng. They'd smile and pretend everything was perfect when it was far from it. That they weren't at loggerheads over their future.

With a curse he slammed a fist against the panel, frustrated, angry that she'd let fear come between them. That she'd kept so much from him.

From this moment on, he would do all in his power to convince her that their marriage was more important than anything. He would somehow vanquish her fears.

* * *

Leila stayed in the shower until her skin threatened to pucker, letting the temperature go from a soothing warm to a bracing chill in hope that the cold would ease the puffiness her crying had surely created.

Her thoughts were a jumble of wanting him. Loving him. Yet his demands veered into unreasonable. What happened to the carefree man she'd picnicked with today? The question eluded her as she stepped from the shower.

She hadn't expected Rafael would be there waiting to take her place, waiting to hand her a thirsty towel. Waiting there gloriously naked and aroused with a look of intense need carved on his handsome face.

Her breath seized as his hungry gaze swept over her, his expression so hot that she felt the water droplets sizzle on her wet skin. But his eyes soon narrowed, staring deeply into hers as if suspecting she still held a secret from him.

His distrust sent a glacial shaft spearing through her, freezing any desire that had quickly kindled to life.

Without a word, Leila grabbed the towel and escaped into the bedroom. But she couldn't stop shaking until she heard the blast of water hit the marble enclosure. Couldn't calm the rapid pounding of her heart until she'd dropped on the bed and dragged air into her lungs.

She was in no mood to party, but to stay here would likely prompt Rafael to do the same and right now she couldn't go through another round of intense questioning about their future.

So she went about her toilet mechanically. She dried her hair. She donned her red gown—a strapless creation from an up-and-coming new designer, and try as she might, she couldn't get the memory of Rafael's glorious body from her mind.

But right on its heels remained the biting words they'd

exchanged. The truths they'd revealed. The soft challenges they'd each issued.

Why on earth had she told Rafael that he might be better off without her and their dream? What would she do if he decided she was right? If he walked out of her life?

By the time the water cut off in the shower, she was applying her makeup but was nowhere near calm. How could she be when Rafael was just on the other side of a partition wall, either naked or nearly so as he readied himself for tonight's events?

Leila couldn't be at ease, not as long as she and Rafael were at loggerheads.

She was no longer the young ingenue. She no longer had the fat fortune to squander, having used much of her money to fund her free clinic for young girls with eating disorders. Poor girls like she'd been with little hope of bettering their lives. Girls who starved themselves in the hopes that they'd fit in.

With the last of her makeup expertly applied to where it looked as if she wasn't wearing any at all, she dabbed the perfume she was promoting between her breasts, at her nape and on her wrists. The heady fragrance warmed on her skin, the intensity of it more pronounced, more haunting, than its name.

"Have I ever told you I hate wearing a tux?" Rafael said as he stepped into the bedroom.

"Yes, every time we've attended a black-tie event."

She smiled and reached for the diamond Y necklace Rafael had given her for Christmas last year, a gift that had been delivered to her holiday shoot in Italy by courier. She'd been shocked by his extravagance, yet deeply touched by the gift and the accompanying note.

She'd called him immediately to thank him, and had been relieved to know he'd liked the watch she'd given him.

And during that brief conversation she'd felt suddenly sad and alone, for being apart from the man she loved was no way to spend a holiday.

Shoving that sad fact from her mind, she concentrated on securing the clasp, on the feel of the platinum and diamonds against her skin. This would be the first time she'd worn it, and the weight and size of the pendant was perfect, the blue and brilliant diamonds near blinding when the light hit them just right.

After adding diamond earrings that dangled along her neck, she turned to where she'd dropped her shoes. And her heart nearly stopped beating.

Her imagination didn't begin to capture the raw power and indisputable status of her husband. He could easily go toe to toe with any of the top male models with his devastating good looks, exquisite physique and unhurried predatory stride that brought all that pent-up need coursing back to the surface.

His dark wavy hair was slicked back to reveal a strong profile that was classic and intense. If he'd just stop scowling...

Her gaze dropped to his hands, busily fumbling to fasten his tie. He was making a knotted mess of it, and that realization brought back old memories of her helping him with this task many times before.

Clearly he'd yet to master it! That fact popped the tension that had bubbled up in her earlier.

She slipped her feet into her stilettos, crossed to him and pushed his hands aside. "Let me help you before you strangle yourself."

He flung his arms to the side, his expression one of fierce self-disgust. "Whoever invented a bow tie should be hanged."

She tried not to smile but her lips twitched anyway, for she'd never seen her strong powerful husband become so flustered over something as simple as a tie. She made quick work of loosening the knots and starting over. In less than a minute she'd fastened the perfect bow for him.

"There," she said, giving his muscled chest a pat.

With effort she stepped back from him, for one pat called for two. One more lingering touch. Like a caress.

He turned to the mirror but his fierce scowl didn't lessen a fraction. "You always make this look so simple."

"It's really not that complicated. A shoot I was on long ago required me to remove a gentleman's tie and put it on," she said. "Since we had to do many sessions to get it right, the lesson stuck with me."

"You undressed a gentleman?"

"I took his tie off," she said, surprised Rafael was still jealous of her.

"How did I miss that ad?"

It took her a moment to realize he wasn't joking. That realization totally blew her away, for it implied that he'd seen the bulk of her spreads. That he had taken an interest in what she'd done.

The lesson of learning to tie a proper bow was all but forgotten, for it had transpired in the waning days of her reign as the waif model. Back when she was a victim of anorexia, barely eating enough to stay alive in a desperate attempt to stop her bosom from expanding and her hips from rounding.

If she hadn't been so naive, perhaps she would have realized that her efforts were in vain. That all she would accomplish would be to jeopardize her health.

She'd had a lot to think about during her long recovery—a lot to learn about herself and her controlling mother. Her road to recovery had been arduous and doubts about her ability to stage a successful comeback had plagued her night and day.

But she'd pushed forward. She'd fired the agent who had listened to Leila's mother instead of her, and she began ignoring her mother's demands.

With her new curves and determination, she set her sights on becoming the next hot model that woman ached to emulate and men longed to bed. But she hadn't realized she'd truly succeeded as a woman until she'd met Rafael.

She glanced at him under the sweep of her lashes. Such a handsome man. Such a determined one.

He'd made her feel beautiful from that first moment they met. He'd turned her into a sensual woman.

Could he turn her into a mother as well? Dare she hope it was possible to overcome the fear choking her?

Time would tell. She only hoped it didn't run out for them before she could find her inner strength.

The next five days were a grueling repeat of elegant premieres, demanding parties, personal interviews for him and fascinating photo shoots for her. Rafael had never shied away from the limelight or the chance to tout his innovations, but he found little enjoyment doing the same thing over and over.

The days were incredibly long. The nights achingly short and a torment for him to endure.

The king-size bed afforded them ample space, yet in the velvet hush of night he would awake from the sleep he'd finally found when she would curl up against him. Any of those nights he could have taken her, aroused her with hot kisses and hotter caresses until she begged for his possession.

But he wouldn't take her by surprise. He wanted her awake. Willing. Wanting him as much as he wanted her. So far that hadn't happened. So far they hadn't gone beyond a few kisses, hot caresses and scorching looks.

But then her demanding schedule exhausted her. He'd seen it in her eyes, in the weary steps she took once they were in their room alone.

He knew she needed to get away from the hustle of endless shoots, interviews and the constant expectation of the perfumery to tout their fragrance along with the film. He knew, too, that she wouldn't rest on her own.

So he began stealing time from his schedule so he could whisk her away from the crowds. Time hadn't allowed them to do more than slip away for a few hours. Shopping. Sightseeing. And occasionally indulging in a tempting dessert at one of the many cafés which he considered a personal boon.

Because today was the last of her shoots, he'd driven them to Nice where they'd dined on a Provençal dinner of salt-crusted sea bass served with a violet artichoke salad.

For dessert, he ordered a tiramisu that he and Leila were sharing, just as they'd done when they were young lovers. When sharing was all he could afford and only then just barely.

"You are a very bad influence on me," she said as she took another taste of the feather-light dessert, her lips closing around the silver spoon while her eyes closed in what was clearly gastronomic ecstasy.

"I am a good influence on you, because I let you be yourself, *querida*," he said, and they both knew it was the truth whether she would admit it or not.

She smiled and looked away, but not before he caught the glimpse of sadness in her hazel eyes. He knew before she spoke that their lighthearted jaunt was ending.

"My agent told me during the last wardrobe change that I have been offered a contract with a top designer to be their model for their spring selection," she said. "It's a fabulous opportunity that I was afraid I wouldn't land."

He waited for her to expound, to say how much she regretted having to turn them down, before he realized the obvious. "You've accepted the offer."

"Yes. My agent and I will have to go over details point by point before I sign," she said, excitement ringing in her voice, "but we're tentatively scheduled to begin shooting in a little over a month."

Damn! He'd been afraid something like this would happen, that a designer or company would dangle the right carrot in front of her to tempt her from him again.

But he'd also thought she was already contracted for a shoot after the film festival and asked her just that.

"I was, but it was with a local designer and would only have lasted a couple of days," she said, carefully folding her linen and laying it beside her place. "This offer exceeds anything that has been sent my way in far too long. The profits from it alone will establish a trust that will keep the free clinic afloat in lean times."

The clinic! That was clearly where her heart rested.

It was quite obvious to him that she'd jumped at this chance, not for the small fortune she'd make but for the escape it offered her.

The hazy picture of family that had begun to form in his mind blurred to gray. The pinch of profound loneliness that had tormented him since childhood grew into a hollow ache. Would he forever be without family? A real home? Love?

Rafael shrugged into his jacket, his anger and hurt banked under a careful mask. "Congratulations."

"Thank you."

His hungry gaze swept over his breathtakingly gorgeous wife, and his blood heated. He had waited long enough. They might not be starting a family now, but he wanted her in his bed. And he'd have her there tonight.

* * *

The premiere of an animated feature must have been charming, for the majority of the audience laughed uproariously. But Rafael found it difficult to concentrate on anything but the woman beside him.

When he'd gone to Aruba to join her in March, he'd hoped they could start their family then. Of course he'd had no idea she'd suffered a miscarriage six months earlier, that she was nowhere physically or mentally near ready to begin a family.

"Is that all you think of anymore?" she'd asked as they lay together replete after their lovemaking.

It had been his main train of thought for far longer than he cared to admit, and for the life of him, he hadn't been able to explain the restlessness in him. He just ached to have that close connection, which he'd been denied as a child, with someone.

The past year had been a chaotic yet lonely grind. He'd realized then just how much he missed and loved Leila. How much he wanted to move their marriage to the next level. Family.

"I am tired of living like we do, Leila," he'd said at last. "We didn't even spend Christmas together this year."

"I was on a shoot," she'd said. "You could have joined me."

And he might have, but he hadn't known anything about it until the last minute. By then he'd already promised his mother he'd help her deliver much-needed supplies to the São Paulo poor marooned in the mountains. He'd not disappoint her or the children, for the memory of being on the receiving end of charity was never far from his mind.

"Your schedule is always so full, as is mine. There is hardly time for us anymore," he'd said, annoyed that his own career kept him from his beloved wife.

He'd reached across and took her hand, entwining his

fingers with hers, savoring the jolt of awareness that always ripped through him with they touched.

"We'll have a week together in France, and though the days will be hectic, the nights will be ours."

"Yes," she said, speaking to his throat instead of meeting his eyes. "We can talk about it then."

He'd wanted to argue the point, to get her to commit. But the fact remained he'd gone eight long months without seeing his wife. Without holding her. Kissing her. Making love to her until they both fell into an exhausted sleep.

But the elation that had surged through him after adoring her with his hands, mouth and body had been shattered when he'd asked her to accompany him to his brother's wedding the following week. She'd refused, claiming she couldn't postpone an upcoming shoot. Perhaps that was true, but she'd made no attempt to even try.

She had chosen her career over him and his family.

Rafael blinked as the score blared in the theater and the final credits began rolling on the film. He couldn't believe it was over. Just like he didn't want to believe this week with Leila was nearly at an end.

"Which party do you wish to attend first?" he asked as they left the cinema, their movement slowed by the crush of celebrities and the inevitable waiting as pictures were taken on the red carpet.

"Actually, I'd prefer to return to the suite. It's been a long day."

"Then that is what we will do."

"You don't have to leave the parties just because I am," she said.

He took her hand, struck with a sense of bittersweet failure. Yet another need pulsed hot and heavy in him too.

"I've grown bored with the parties, *querida*. I'd rather spend this night with you."

She pressed a hand to his chest and her wide eyes met his. He read uncertainty, fatigue and something he couldn't place in those most celebrated hazel orbs.

"You're sure you won't regret leaving the gaiety?"

"Positive."

There would always be parties. But his week with Leila would be over soon. Too soon.

He fully intended to make the most of their remaining time together. Wanted this night with her without further arguing. A night filled with nothing but lovemaking so he could brand each second on his memory.

"I want you, Leila."

"Then let's get out of here."

CHAPTER SIX

RAFAEL'S blood was on fire as he skirted the crowd as quickly as possible, his fingers entwined with Leila's. They reached their suite in less than ten minutes, though it felt as if hours had crawled by.

He swept them into the room and locked the door, heart thundering in his chest. Her fragrance was totally erotic, mingling with her own musk to drive him wild with desire.

His mouth came down on hers. Hard. Demanding. Savage in intensity, in raw primal need.

She slid her arms around his neck and strained against him, her kiss ripe with promise and passion. She tasted of honey and lemon.

A deep growl of satisfaction ripped from him. His mouth left hers to trail kisses down her slender neck, laving, nipping, reveling in the sultry mewls she made, the desperate way she clutched at him.

He stepped back just enough so he could cup her breasts, lifting them until they nearly spilled over the top of her low strapless dress. They seemed fuller, tighter, and he was suddenly thankful for those five kilograms she'd grudgingly gained.

His head bent to taste one silken globe, nuzzling her dress down to bare her to the waist. He swirled his tongue around one taut nipple before he sucked hard on it.

"Yes," she moaned, her fingernails raking his back, her spine bowed to press her breasts closer to his mouth.

Heart hammering in his chest, he suckled her hard, nipping at her, then laving. It seemed an eternity had passed since they'd made love in March.

A lifetime of wanting her. Dreaming of her. Now she was in his arms. Now he'd take his time with her, he thought, drawing deeply on one breast and then the other until they gleamed with moisture, until the nipples were hard and rosy.

Until she quivered in his arms and his arousal had grown painful.

"I can't take it." She grasped both ends of his tie and pulled him into the bedroom, back to the enormous bed.

A tremor rocketed through him, far stronger than he'd ever felt before. He was nearly blind with lust now as he pushed her red dress to the floor and stared at her, clad only in a sheer crimson thong. Perfection. Her breasts were high and firm, her waist slender, her hips rounded just enough to be feminine.

"Please," she said, rubbing against him, her fingers desperately trying to loosen the studs on his shirt.

"With pleasure."

He picked her up and tossed her on the bed, then hooked his thumbs under her thong and yanked it off, eliciting a startled squeak from her. "You are exquisite."

"And you are overdressed," she said, her smile a beckoning taunt of tease and passion.

"Vixen."

He tore off his clothes and fell on her, pressing them both into the sumptuous mattress. Their lips met in a maelstrom of passion, tongues dueling in slick, strong thrusts that left him hard and aching, teeth nipping with erotic intent to make her gasp and purr in turn.

His hands were all over her, memorizing the thrusts of her breasts, the tautness of her nipples that he tasted and tormented until she cried out again.

She glided her hands down his back, her fingers digging into his buttocks to hold him close even as she arched against him, grinding her pelvis against his length. Was she as desperate as he to be inside her?

He slipped a hand between them to find her slick folds were plump with desire, wet from wanting him. His body hardened more, jolting now with the need to drive himself into her. To take her now and be done with it, then take her again and again until they were both too tired to move.

Lust pounded through his veins in hot surges as he pressed his mouth to her flat belly, sliding lower to the caramel curls damp with desire. God, how he'd missed this with her.

"Rafael," she whispered, her voice low and throaty, her hands clutching his head.

He slid his palms up her inner thighs and pushed her legs apart, baring her to him. In March, the sex between them had been fast. Fierce. The second time had been just as urgent.

This time he would savor her, give them both what they craved. He settled between her creamy thighs, his palms cupping her tight buttocks as he bent to press one hot kiss on her tender flesh.

She cried out, her back bowing, her fingers holding his head at the apex of her quivering thighs. He emitted a low growl and speared into her with his tongue, tasting her, seeking the sweet spot that would drive her wild for him.

There was no finesse now, just primal instinct as his mouth tasted and tormented her hot swollen nub again and again.

His heart hammered as his tongue mimicked what the

hard length of his sex ached to do. He felt the tension coiling in her, felt her tremble beneath him, felt himself growing hard as a rock.

He groaned as his body did the same, as if there were an invisible thread between them that pulled them both taut. That bound them together forever.

Ruthlessly shoving that fact to the back of his mind, he channeled his thoughts on pleasuring Leila. He wanted her to remember every erotic stroke, every ravenous kiss, every thrust of his tongue and fingers and sex, when this week ended.

He wanted her to wake in the night and ache to be with him instead of on a shoot at some barren location. He wanted her to think of him and the family they should be starting instead of her career.

His fingers slipped inside her silken core, thrusting harder, giving him that opportunity to watch passion sweep over her in a rosy flush, see her open just for him. Her inner muscles clamped down hard on his fingers even as tremors shot through her.

Her head thrashed on the pillow, eyes pinched shut, incoherent sounds bubbling from her. Sweat beaded his forehead and slicked his back.

He hurt from holding his own need back. But in this, he refused to be selfish, for her pleasure made his all the more intense.

When her climax finally came, it swept over her in one long shuttering cry that sang through his blood. She pressed her head into the mattress and went stiff, his name bursting from her in a reedy litany.

Nothing could be more beautiful than watching her now. No woman was as giving of herself. No woman could ever be this trusting in his arms.

If she could only extend that to him outside the bedroom…

With a savage growl, he surged into her with one long powerful thrust, her spasms pulling him in deeper. So deep he felt the burn of her flesh against his own, felt her passion sear him from the inside out.

They reached their climax together in a glittering burst of color that rivaled the display of fireworks on the beach.

His name burst from her lips. This was perfect. Nirvana.

In the aftermath of such an explosive joining, they sprawled on the bed, spent. Sated.

They dozed. Then they woke to explore each other at leisure in the dark of the night.

They made love again, slowly, drawing it out until they couldn't stand the wait another moment. And somewhere in the wee hours of the morning they finally fell asleep in each other's arms.

Leila came awake slowly, caught somewhere between lusty dreams of Rafael and that state of confusion of not quite remembering the day, the time. His spicy scent clung to her skin, to the bed coverings, proving their sex had been real.

She stretched in the bed and turned to Rafael, her body protesting the workout. Her welcoming smile vanished as she stared at the empty bed.

Memories of March rushed back to her, of him leaving their bed without a goodbye. Without even a damned note.

Her hand swept over the pillow and over the place he would have slept. It was cool. The suite was quiet and dark.

He wouldn't leave. Wouldn't leave her like this again. Would he?

And then she heard it. The creak of a chair in the salon. She scrambled from the bed, gathering the bedsheet as she did. Her heart felt as if a vise were squeezing it. She had to remind herself to breathe.

Leila stepped from the bedroom and scanned the salon. She sagged against the doorjamb, nearly weak with relief.

Rafael sat at the desk, his fingers flying over the silent touch pad on his innovative laptop. He wore khaki shorts and nothing else. His hair was mussed. The broad bronzed width of his shoulders racked tight as he concentrated.

"What time did you get up?" she asked.

He whipped around, seeming startled that she was there. "An hour or so ago. I received an urgent text regarding the integrated graphics on the new phone."

She knew from the early days of their marriage that he'd spend long hours poring over such problems. She knew, too, that he would not rest until he'd found a solution.

"You'll be busy working all day, then," she said, disappointed to have their last day in France disrupted.

"No. I have isolated the problem and sent details back to my manager already."

"Wonderful."

His response was a clipped nod.

The awkward moment stretched out when she wondered at his thoughts, when concern skipped along her nerves. "Is something wrong?"

He frowned, his gaze sweeping down her body. But when his eyes met hers again, she couldn't read anything in their glittering black depths.

"Would you like me to order room service?"

"Please, I'm hungry."

He pushed to his feet and padded toward her, his stride long and graceful. This time a slow smile curved the beautifully chiseled contour of his mouth. "Do you have anything scheduled this afternoon?"

She shook her head as a different hunger swelled within her. "Nothing. Do you have something in mind?"

He leaned over her and trailed one finger along her cheek, across her lips. She tipped her head back as that same finger glided down her throat.

"I want to make love with you," he said, tugging the sheet free.

Before it hit the ground, she was in his arms.

That's where she stayed for the rest of the afternoon. In bed. On the sofa. In the shower.

They ate a light breakfast, feeding each other. They played, they laughed and they loved. And when the afternoon bled into night, Leila mourned that this week with Rafael was now over.

And she dreaded what tomorrow's parting would bring.

Leila walked down the hall toward their room on a wave of giddy excitement. The festival ended tonight with the awards ceremony, and she knew that Rafael was exceptionally proud of Nathaniel for winning the prized trophy for his directing of *Carnival*.

It was a total departure from the films Nathaniel had starred in thus far. The indie film was also the first one made by Nathaniel's and Rafael's fledgling production company formed in order to make this movie, a gritty urban thriller set in Rio.

The rags-to-riches flick had left Leila shaken and stunned, for the film spoke to her deeply as she, too, had started with nothing, escaping poverty in the *favelas*.

It also confirmed that she and Rafael had something profoundly in common, for only someone who understood the plight of the desperately poor Brazilians trapped in the violent slums could depict the raw emotion and angst on film with such heart-wrenching detail. It made her love Rafael even more.

She'd longed to quiz him on the details but she held back when he waved aside any accolades as they had left the theater. If he didn't wish to talk about how he knew exactly how life in the slums were, she would not press him.

"I just contributed money," Rafael said when congratulated for the award. "Nathaniel did all the work."

An exaggeration she was sure. But since he declined attending the many parties that would reign on the yachts and in the clubs up and down La Croisette until the wee hours of the morning, all touting the brilliance of the film, she kept her questions to herself.

As Nathaniel and his wife did the same, even bowing gracefully out of having dinner with them tonight, she was even more sure that this movie had a far deeper and personal meaning for the half brothers. That alone troubled her, for it made her wonder what their childhood had really been like.

Rafael had never divulged much, even when she'd asked. She certainly wasn't about to pry now, for he'd been in an odd mood since the film ended.

And in truth, she was relieved that Rafael hadn't made other arrangements for them tonight. She longed to return to their room, to spend this final night with him alone like they had last night. But she dreaded that he would press her for her decision on a family again, and that this might be the end of their marriage. She simply couldn't deal with that now.

She chanced a peek at him and her breath caught. The chiseled lines of his face seemed more intense, his eyes darker and more troubled. Was he thinking that their idyll was drawing to an end too?

God knew the precious moments in Rafael's arms were

without compare for her. There just hadn't been enough of them at this festival. Now it was nearly over, and she couldn't ignore that niggling of doubt that he was already pulling away from her.

"So what are your plans after the festival?" she asked, sliding her long silk scarf from around her neck and letting it trail behind her.

"There are things I need to attend to in Brazil," he said, closing the door behind him, shutting out the world again, shutting them in for one last night.

She faced him then, noting the tension that had gripped him during the film was still in force, still creating an invisible wall between then. "More trouble with your business?"

"No, that's under control now." He shrugged out of his tuxedo jacket and flung it on a chair, his expression as taut as the tension now humming in the room. "I've neglected the *fazenda* of late."

He owned a farm? In the early days of their marriage that was all he'd talked about—building a home for them away from the city. A place where they could escape the rigors of their careers. Where they could raise a family in peace.

It had been the dream she'd held as well, until she'd lost their child. Until she'd realized that the hope of having a real family might be far beyond her reach.

"You've bought a house, then?" she asked, trying to sound conversational and light when she was hurt that he'd never told her he'd moved forward with their dream home. "Tell me about it."

He crossed to the balcony and threw open the door to admit the welcoming salt-tinged breeze. "The land is rich and producing fine crops, and the staff is smaller but above par. I trust you will approve."

"I'm sure I will," she said, then wondered when she'd get the chance to go. Certainly not in the next month or so.

He glanced back at her, his smile relaxed, though there was a pensive set to his mouth that kept her from feeling at ease. "It is a typical farm *casa* with large airy rooms. There is space for you to have an office if you wish. I had one built for my needs."

"Ultrahigh-tech?"

"It is what I do," he said with pride.

And her own pride stung, for while he would never give up his career or even partial control of it, he expected her to embrace full-time motherhood.

She waited for him to go on, to tell her more about the house he'd dreamed of building one day for them. Of the bedroom they'd share, and the nursery he was intent on filling.

But he simply resumed his study of the sea, both hands braced on the jamb, his white shirt stretching tight over his muscular back. And maybe that was for the best, for the last thing she wanted to do now was engage in another discussion about starting their family.

Leila pulled her scarf through her hand again and again as unease crackled along her nerves. "What time is your flight tomorrow?"

"Seven in the morning."

Her plane didn't depart until eleven. Though she'd hoped they could travel to the airport together, she didn't wish to spend hours there waiting for her flight.

"I suppose you should get some rest now," she said, feeling awkward when she longed to blurt out her needs.

"I can sleep on the plane, *querida*." He turned to face her this time, and the need in his gaze reached out to her, stroked her desire and sent a hum of want crashing through her.

She shook her head, afraid this easy mood would be broken. "Good, because I need you tonight."

"And I need you, Leila," he said, his smile sad. "I hope one day you'll realize just how much."

Leila walked up to him, noting the catch in his breath, the flaring of his nostrils, the darkening tinge on his cheeks. She looped her scarf around his neck and gave it a tug, and passion exploded in his dark eyes.

"Show me how much," she said, giving the scarf a hard tug.

CHAPTER SEVEN

RAFAEL set his teeth. It was damned near impossible to resist her when her eyes were blazing with desire. And why should he when this was their last night together?

With an erotic growl, his mouth swooped down on hers. The kiss was a consuming fire, but Leila welcomed the heat, for she could taste his passion, feel his need pulse in his muscles and vibrate into her on a dulcet sigh.

She raked her fingernails down his back and held on tight as he backed her up against the wall. He let out a primal hiss, his pelvis grinding against hers. His tongue plundered, retreated and staked claim to her mouth again.

"I don't want this week to end," she said, her fingers making short work of freeing his gorgeous length from his trousers, wanting him in her, desperate to hold on to him any way she could, for something had shifted in their relationship yet again, something that threatened to pull him from her.

"It doesn't have to," he said, his voice gruff with hope.

Had he finally succeeded in reaching her?

The thought of returning to the empty penthouse or the *casa* sickened him. He was so damned tired of living alone. He selfishly yearned for his wife in his arms and his life.

She claimed she felt the same, yet for all her protestations she was still placing her career first.

The thought went up in flames as she scraped her hands over his chest, and he marveled that he didn't see sparks crackling in the dim light of the room. He was on fire for her, consumed with need.

He shoved her gown to her waist with one hand and snapped the thin strap of her thong with the other, the near-violent action more titillating than she could have imagined.

She kicked what remained of her panties free in a desperate rush to get rid of the encumbrance.

He growled his approval and lifted her by her waist, holding her against the wall for a heartbeat before he brought her down on his thick hot length. Sparks of passion rocketed through her.

She cried out and wrapped her legs around his lean hips, clutching him tightly to her, her face buried against his neck as that first wave of sensations tore through her. Her head spun from the sheer power of him inside her, making them one again.

Her heart thudded strong and she wished this would go on forever.

He hissed out a breath and shuttered, going still as if he, too, had nearly passed out from this explosive joining, as if savoring every quiver of flesh against flesh, every slick sweet glide within. As if he were afraid to move for fear it would shatter to pieces.

She clung to him, focused on his pulse pounding through her in an erotic beat that made her heart sing. Her muscles stretched to accommodate his length before instinctively tightening around him to milk him—draw out all he could give her. Hold him tight, as if by doing so she'd never lose this moment. Never lose him.

"Meu amor," he said, pulling nearly out of her before slamming back in where he belonged. His mouth came

down on hers, the kiss as greedy as the need gnawing away inside her.

She threaded her fingers through his thick hair and ground her mouth against his even as her pelvis moved against him, matching his thrusts, his passion. She kissed him deeply, determined to leave no doubt in his mind that he was her only lover. That he was her love.

They broke apart on a gasp, desperate to draw air into lungs that burned. Her skin was on fire now, the blaze within her so hot and fierce that she was certain this time the heat would consume them.

He tossed his head back, his features cast in bold relief, an erotic deity come to life, the emotions stark and clear. Passion. Pain. Possession.

He controlled the moment. Controlled her with an iron will that left her panting for more, that left her at his mercy.

She couldn't have continued her sensual assault a moment longer. Raw passion crashed through her with the force of a tidal wave, sweeping her away on a wave of bliss.

Every inch of her was ultrasensitized, from the aching tips of her breasts that drilled into his chest to her heart that pounded in time to his—hard, fast. Wanting more. Wanting all he could give her. Wanting to hold this moment forever.

She lifted her head and stared into eyes that smoldered with black flames of passion, so intense she trembled as the carnal fire licked through her veins. She burned deep inside, forever branded by his passion, her skin so sensitized that the slight abrasion of his fingers stroking her quivering body was sweet torture.

They had made love every way imaginable, but never with this explosive passion. Never this intense and consuming. Never so powerful that she actually thought if she died now, she would die blissfully happy.

Her trembling hands stroked down his powerful back

that quivered at her touch. She pinched her eyes shut, imbedding this joining on her memory, for surely she wanted this moment to last forever, to hold him in her arms, in her body, until the end of time.

For when they were locked in love, the world faded into oblivion. She focused on him moving on her, in her. They were one, their breaths mingling, their hearts pounding in tandem to a sensual melody only they could hear.

The pressure inside her was cataclysmic, propelling her into the stratosphere. She gasped and reached toward that crystalline brilliance of completion just out of her reach. A place where she could only feel and not think. A nirvana where she simply lay sated in exquisite splendor.

With Rafael.

If he wasn't with her, she couldn't go.

She held him tighter, determined to take him with her into her glorious climax. But that was ripped from her as her body splintered with sensation, trembling, tossing her up among the stars.

She screamed his name and reached for him, their entwined fingers her lifeline that surged with a maelstrom of passion. But that, too, grew dim, a ghost image that was beautiful to see, a memory that was seared on her soul.

She was dimly aware of his body straining against her own, her body pressed against the cool wall. Of his final thrust as he reached his climax with a hoarse shout that made her smile, for she'd given him all she had to offer.

It was much later that her brain began to function, when the ruckus from the beach and the clubs became an intrusion on this special moment. She rested lax in the cradle of his embrace, the wall cold and unyielding against her spine, his body hot and hard against her own.

Her arms hung at her sides, her hands free. Her only remaining connection to him now was that he was still buried deeply inside her. But that, too, ended as he slowly eased out of her.

"That was incredible," she said, pressing a kiss against his damp chest and smiling as his skin puckered against her lips.

"You are incredible," he said, his hands curling over her bare bottom and simply holding her close.

She glided her palms up his arms to his damp shoulders, lifting her head from where she'd pillowed it on his chest to look at his face. "If I am, it is only because of you, my love."

"Everything ends eventually," he said, the note of finality in his tone threatening to dim her joy. "Then new memories can be made."

She took a relieved breath and pressed her mouth to his, grazing his lips once, twice. "Then let's make new memories tonight."

His big body tensed a fraction, and for a heartbeat she feared he'd refuse. What would she do then?

"You know what I want, Leila," he said.

She took a breath. Then another. But in the end she couldn't lie.

"I know, but I fear I might never be able to give you that, Rafael."

Rafael swore under his breath. There was no joy in knowing nothing had changed. In knowing that Leila did not trust him enough to help her overcome her fears. He was torturing himself by making love with her, knowing she'd go her way in the morning, in control of her life, but alone.

His mouth closed over hers, not with brutal passion or driving lust but a gentle kiss that made his soul sing even as his heart clenched over at his failure to make his marriage work. At his failure to make his beautiful wife see the future they could have together, if only she would trust him.

He selfishly wanted more memories of her to hold long afterward even though that would be a torment to his soul as well. He wanted this night. Wanted all she could give him, as little as that was.

Regrets and guilt could torment him tomorrow. Tonight was theirs.

He tore his mouth from hers and she mewled a protest, pressing her mouth to his throat instead, nipping, laving, moving down his chest to suckle his skin.

Desire bolted through him like lightning. His sex jolted and snapped taut.

"You are insatiable," he said thickly, giving her bare bottom a squeeze that brought her body pressing tightly against him again.

Such exquisite torment!

"But you like me that way," she said, her voice a throaty purr again.

It was true. He liked that she wasn't shy in bed with him. That she knew what pleased him, what made their pleasure all the more memorable.

If only he could calm her fears about motherhood now. How ironic that in the early days of their marriage, he'd been afraid that he'd not be a fit father, just like his own. His greatest fear was that his father's evil would eventually come out in him, that he'd somehow turn into the monster who could turn his back on his own flesh and blood. Who could inflict pain with a cruel smile. That his life was too busy to be burdened with children yet.

It had been his suggestion to put off having a family in the early days, sure that he lacked the patience to deal with the bonds of parenthood when his marriage was so new. When he was still at the beginnings of launching his career.

Yet just two years into marriage and the lonely ache in him had expanded. He'd realized that he needed Leila to make him whole. To ground him. To complete him. His desire to be with her and start a family with her had overwhelmed him.

He and his siblings had little contact. His mother was deeply involved helping the indigenous people, a cause he supported.

But he had vowed to keep his yearnings to himself until their third anniversary. His and Leila's careers were at crucial stages and he understood and respected that. But each day he had poured his heart into his work, and each night he had come home to a cold empty house.

He was miserable. He missed Leila terribly and he dreamed of her having his babies. Ached to spend every day and night with her, and the ache to have his own family had nearly consumed him.

But Leila wasn't ready. She may never be. He had to give her space, maybe let her go forever.

"Join me in Malibu," she said, tracing his jaw with a fingernail.

"I'm tied up in Brazil for the next month."

"Rio after that, then?"

"Yes, we'll spend the next months back home."

"That sounds good."

Rafael tightened his hold on her and strode into the bedroom, his mind too fogged with passion to think logically now.

He longed to lie beside her, cover her, have her straddle him. He'd adore her with his hands and lips and tongue until they could no longer move. Until they were sated in body and spirit.

"You will be exhausted in the morning," he promised as he stretched out beside her on the bed.

"As will you."

He smiled at that, for she was right. But he craved that sweet exhaustion. He wanted to leave knowing he'd given her all the pleasure that he could. He wanted her to wake in the night and miss him being beside her.

"I will hold you to that promise, *querida*."

"As long as you hold me."

He would do that and more. Much, much more.

He splayed a hand on her flat belly and smiled as her silken skin quivered beneath his palm, the flesh warm. Smooth. Perfection.

"Make love with me," she said, reaching for him.

"With pleasure."

His fingers brushed through the carefully trimmed hair at the apex of her thighs and she shifted, lifting her hips in silent invitation. His lips captured hers in a kiss that commanded and teased in turn. He bit her full lower lip, then laved the swollen flesh even as his fingers toyed with the plump folds between her thighs.

"Please," she said, digging her fingernails into his sides to bring him closer, setting his skin on fire with her passion. "Hurry."

But he was in no rush to see these last hours slip away. He'd pleasure her with care. He'd savor every second she remained in his arms, for it could be months before he saw her again.

"Beautiful," he whispered as he trailed kisses down her neck, taking love bites that made her quiver and send a fresh rush of blood to his already engorged sex. "You were made for loving. You were made for me."

He speared one finger into her hot tight core, groaning that she was as tight and sweet as a virgin still. Sweat popped out on his brow and slicked his back. Blood roared in his ears.

He thrust another finger into her while his thumb found her pleasure point, rubbing hard and fast.

She bucked and cried out, her plea captured in his mouth, branded on his soul.

He would make this last night special for her. For him.

He set a fast tempo, drawing the moment out. His thumb found her pleasure spot and rubbed insistently as his lips captured one tight nipple and suckled hard. He laved each ripe breast until both tightened. His hand rode her hard toward an explosive climax.

He rocked back and watched her, his heart hammering so hard with need he could barely draw a breath, thinking he'd never seen anything as beautiful as Leila lost in passion. Reaching for her climax, coming undone at his touch.

She was free now. Her features open. Natural. More passionate than any professional still shot could convey.

His.

Before the last tremors left her, he settled between her lithe thighs and thrust into her quivering heat with a husky shout of completion. She clutched him to her with her arms, her core muscles, her sultry eyes gleaming like cut ambers.

Sweet, sweet oblivion called to him, yet he moved with slow deliberation, drawing this moment out, committing this to memory. Her nails raked down his back creating rivers of fire. Her long lean legs wrapped around his hips, holding him close, demanding his all.

He gritted his teeth, pumping into her, fingers twined now, eyes locked on each other. "Remember this," he charged, driving into her hard, fast, pushing her into the stars that surely glittered just for her.

"Always," she said, her voice no more than a breath.

Then she was lost, her body trembling as her climax overcame her. He sank into her once more and let himself go, lost in the flickering carnival lights of passion with her.

The last thing Rafael wanted to see was the dawn of a new day. But it came anyway.

He rolled from the bed without waking her and took a shower, but the pounding spray failed to ease the tension gripping him this morning. Last night was a clear poignant memory.

Now it was over.

He dressed, then stood by the bed, watching her sleep. He'd promised he'd wake her before he left, but what was the use in depriving her of much-needed sleep?

"I will miss you, *querida*," he whispered.

Then with a heavy heart, he slipped from the suite.

CHAPTER EIGHT

NEARLY two weeks had passed since they'd parted in France and still Leila had to struggle to find the strength to get out of bed each morning. Even the tranquility she felt at her home perched high in the Malibu hills was absent this time.

Part of that was because for the first time ever she'd had great difficulty falling asleep to the soothing wash of the tide. But most of her anxiety could be blamed on her heartache over being apart from Rafael.

What little rest she got was fitful—plagued with images of him loving her, his arms open for her return. Him asking her what she wanted most—her career or a family.

Dammit, she wanted both. But her fear over one drove her full tilt into pursuing the other.

Perhaps that was the reason she'd seen a return of the nightmares that had tormented her after her miscarriage.

If she hadn't received such favorable reports from the clinic regarding a critically young girl who'd reminded her of herself at that age, she'd have found it difficult to function at all. But the money spent on the girl's care was worth the heartache—worth the sacrifice. At least, that's what she tried to tell herself.

"You've put in horribly long hours this past month," her agent said when Leila finally confessed she was worried about her stamina. "I'm concerned with your exhaustion. It's showing on your face and that won't do."

Leila was well aware of that! As exhausted as she was, she'd never be able to keep up with the demands expected of her when the real work began.

"Have you seen a doctor?" her agent asked.

"No. When do you expect them to send over a contract?"

"Any day now," her agent said, frowning again as if annoyed that she'd changed the subject. "Once you sign, they'll want you to be ready to work. It would be crushing to your career if you fell off schedule and were unable to work. Or worse, if you go there looking as exhausted as you do."

A model's nightmare. And at her age, maintaining a youthful look was crucial. She had to do something, and if it meant taking medicine for depression again, then that's what she'd do.

"Very well," Leila said. "I'll ring my physician today."

But due to her doctor's busy schedule and Leila's celebrity status he agreed to see her after hours.

"Congratulations on being the spokeswoman for *Bare Souls*," her doctor said by way of greeting, proving that even a professional whom she admired for his bluntly honest demeanor was awed by Leila's stellar success. "I trust the festival was as exciting as the video clips of it suggested."

"It was an experience of a lifetime," Leila said, her heart warming over the memory of unbelievable bliss with Rafael. "Unfortunately I caught a bit of a bug there and can't seem to shake it."

The doctor quickly launched into his professional persona. "Tell me what's wrong."

"Exhaustion and a queasy stomach."

"This started in France?"

She frowned. "Actually, I arrived with an upset stomach. At the time I thought I hadn't recovered from a stomach virus."

The doctor patiently listened as she described how food—even the smell of it—would turn her stomach. How she'd feel perfectly fine one moment only to become violently ill the next.

"It didn't last more than a few days and then I felt fine. Except for being tired," she admitted as the doctor gave her a careful examination.

"I'll ask you this once because, considering your medical history, I have to rule it out," the doctor said. "Have you had a relapse with your eating disorder?"

She'd expected the question. "No. I've adhered to a healthy diet and have not been tempted to revert to anorexia once since my recovery. In fact, I have gained weight."

"Good for you," the doctor said after weighing her and announcing she was five pounds heavier than the last visit.

The weight gain shocked her, for though she noticed her clothes fit snugger, this was a much greater increase than she'd ever had. She'd been trying to put weight on, had promised Rafael she would, but she had always believed that this would be impossible for her to actually achieve! She had thought that when she had reached her desired ten kilos extra her first erratic impulse would be to begin an immediate and rigid diet. But she had hardly noticed the gain. It certainly hadn't been at the forefront of her mind.

For a moment she still felt that initial gut impulse to diet, to starve herself if she must, but it wasn't anywhere near as strong as she had feared. Was there hope for her and Rafael and the future they had once dreamed of?

But almost as soon as this joyous feeling settled in Leila's heart, she shook herself. She'd still had a negative reaction to her weight gain, even if only slight. Added to her desolation over her miscarriage, this only confirmed her fears about pregnancy and the belief that she'd never be able to cope with the body changes she'd endure while pregnant. What if she tried, only to fail again? Where would that leave her and Rafael then?

"Leila?" The doctor smiled as she looked up and flushed, embarrassed to be caught lost in internal thought. "Let's focus on what could cause your problems. As for the exhaustion, I imagine your schedule was intense."

"Extremely so."

The passionate nights she'd shared with her husband had cost her much-needed sleep. But she couldn't divulge something that personal, that precious to her.

The doctor frowned and made a few notes. "Yet, you've been tired since the festival ended?"

"Yes. I can't seem to get my energy back no matter how much sleep I get," she said.

"What about rest? Are you having difficulty falling asleep?"

"Yes," she admitted, and because he knew he'd ask more, she simply stated, "I have some personal issues that have troubled me of late, so sleep eludes me."

"How is your mood? Are you depressed?"

"No," she said, though she missed Rafael more than ever before. "But I've had nightmares about my miscarriage again."

The doctor frowned. "Before I give you a prescription for an antidepressant, I want to run blood tests and see if something shows up there. It's very possible you have an infection that is being relentless. If so, the right medicine should set you to rights in no time."

"I hope so. I can't afford to be sick now."

Thirty minutes later, Leila had given blood and urine samples for office tests and was sitting in the empty reception room waiting for preliminary results. Seeing her face on so many magazine covers at once was a shock.

Each one held a variant of the same expression—a woman assured of her status.

Such a lie.

The doctor strode into the waiting room, his expression somewhere between curious and worried. "Leila, are you still taking contraceptives?"

"Faithfully," she said, that query bringing her to her feet.

"You're sure you didn't forget once or twice?"

She shook her head, the first slice of worry scoring her tenuous calm. "Not once."

He rubbed his chin, stretching the moment out. Pulling her already frayed nerves so taut she was sure they'd snap.

"When was the last time you took an anti-biotic?"

"In March," she said. "I was in Aruba on a shoot and the doctor on staff gave me an antibiotic for a urinary tract infection."

He nodded, but his pensive expression kept her on edge. "Did you have intercourse during that time or shortly thereafter?"

She felt her face burn, for that memory, too, was one she would never forget. "Yes. My husband joined me there."

"That explains it."

Her blood turned to ice, chilling her to the bone. "What do you mean, that explains it?"

"Antibiotics can decrease the effectiveness of birth control medicine. Did you use condoms?"

Her cheeks burned hotly from the implications that sprang to mind. And the fear... Dear God, the fear of what was wrong with her was becoming glaringly clear.

I'm on the Pill, she'd said at that tense moment when they were ravenous for each other again. And Rafael had needed no further urging that time or the one following it.

"What's wrong?" she asked the doctor, near frantic now, for his line of questions breathed life into her deepest fears.

"You're pregnant."

Those two words slammed into her with enough force to drop her back in her chair. "I can't be!"

"Yes, you can. The blood tests will tell for sure, but at this point I suspect you are about three months along."

His words sent instant terror crashing through her. She closed her eyes, then snapped them open again, unable to bear the memories of her miscarriage that flashed through her mind. Of losing her precious baby. She couldn't go through that again.

"Oh, my God, this can't be possible!" she said, more to herself than him, hands automatically splayed on her belly.

What an odd twist of fate. While she had been in France, adamantly telling Rafael she didn't feel ready to start a family, she had already been with child.

Rafael would be elated. As she thought of him now and the joy he would feel, her own heart lifted. A baby. Rafael's baby! If only her choking fears would allow her to feel the same intense joy now. If only she could be confident that she and her body would carry this child safely to term. Another fear reared up to send her heart racing. "Can taking the Pill harm my baby?"

"No, but let's suspend it until we get the tests back." Her doctor, always to the point, added, "Leila, having a baby isn't impossible for you, but you will have to take extra precautions because of your history with anorexia. I insist you see a top-notch obstetrician who specializes in high risk."

"Of course." Just like she'd done the last time. And look where that ended. "I'm terrified that I'll have another miscarriage." Or worse, that she'd have a relapse and destroy her baby and herself this time.

The doctor rested a hand on her shoulder, his smile

understanding. "Calm down, Leila. Wait for the blood tests to come back because this could be a false positive."

"All right."

The next twelve hours were sheer hell, but she held her worries inside for most of them, not telling a soul of her fears, her hopes, her worries. Not calling Rafael, for she didn't want to get his hopes up only to have them dashed.

But on the following morning, her agent dropped by with the new contract for her to sign. Of course they were needed immediately.

Leila had no choice but to tell her the truth.

"A pregnancy now could end your career," her agent had said, and though both knew it could signal much more than that, neither brought it up.

"I know that," Leila said. "But if I am pregnant, it'll be another month at least before I'm unable to conceal it. I could work up until I have to bow out."

And if she was pregnant, she would desperately need to hold on to her career, for the baby's sake. She would need the regimen and control she had over that aspect of her life to help her stay relaxed over the changes to her body. And she needed Rafael.

Her agent tapped a mauve fingernail on the contract she'd just delivered. "Maybe I can get them to act fast on this deal and shoot the first round of the campaign before you have to take maternity leave."

"I'd be more than willing to do that," she said, suddenly allowing a glimmer of hope to bloom inside her that there might be a way around this. If only she didn't miscarry this time.

"Right." Her agent didn't sound or look hopeful as she laid the contract on Leila's desk and jotted something on a note. But her next words shocked Leila to the very core. "In the event that you are pregnant, you could always decide to terminate. It's obviously unwanted and unplanned. Here's the name of a good clinic. They've been there for several of my clients. I'll do all I can for you, Leila, but this is your career and your choice to make."

Leila stared blindly at the address her agent handed to her before she jammed the note in her purse. Without a doubt her mother would have insisted she rid herself of a baby that would put her career on hold, just as she'd convinced Leila to be anorexic.

But the very thought of an abortion curdled Leila's stomach. She still had nightmares about her miscarriage. This baby may have been unplanned, but unwanted? Rafael longed for a child and she knew he would make a wonderful father. When she had discovered her pregnancy last time she had been ecstatic at the idea of becoming a mother, of holding her tiny baby in her arms. Then her own body had rejected that baby and the loss of that dream had left her desolate. Purposely ridding herself of her child was unthinkable, and yet she knew if she did carry this child to term a relapse would do the same thing.

"Call me as soon as you get the results," her agent said. "I need to know what you intend to do as soon as possible."

The rest of the day Leila's emotions bounced between fear, hope and despair.

"You're definitely pregnant," her doctor said.

Leila stared out at the waves crashing to the California shore through a sheen of tears. She'd never been more afraid in her life, never wished that Rafael was by her side as much as she did now.

She'd failed her first pregnancy. Had failed both him and their child. But, despite her fear now, she knew she would do everything in her power to protect this one.

"I insist you see an obstetrician," her doctor said. "Shall I arrange it?"

She took a breath and let it out slowly. "Please."

Rafael broke the surface of the clear water and levered himself from the terrace pool. After an exhausting day poring over specs with his IT techs in Rio, he'd returned to his penthouse and headed straight for his private gym.

But even after a grueling workout, he'd not been able to rid himself of the tension that had tied him in knots since he'd left Leila. Even doing countless laps in the pool hadn't beaten the pent-up anger that threatened to consume him over Leila's refusal to face her fears about starting a family.

A part of him was angry with himself too, blamed himself for allowing this terror to take hold of his precious wife. He, more than anyone, understood her concerns, her trepidation. But still in the back of his mind was the old sense of rejection that had tormented him all his life.

His father had refused to acknowledge him. His relationship with his siblings was strong now, yet he had always been the odd one in the group. The bastard.

Even his own mother had spent any precious time they might have had together working for other families. He remembered one Christmas Day when he had been only small and she had dragged him along to help prepare the meal for another family. "It's better this way, for now you will be able to eat a good meal," she'd told him when he'd complained.

But though the leftovers had been excellent, he had been consumed with jealousy as he had watched the other children eat their meal with their parents. Had envied the presents and the laughter and just once had wanted to share such moments with his mother to himself.

But that had rarely happened.

He'd feared he'd always be adrift. Always be the one on the outside looking in at other people's lives.

Then he'd met Leila and his hopes had surged along with his passion and love. Such beautiful plans they'd made. And yet when it came time for them to move their relationship to the next level, when having a family was just within their reach, she was too gripped with fear to try.

She lacked faith in him to believe he'd be there for her, that together they could move mountains. That he'd do whatever was necessary to help her through a pregnancy.

Though she professed she still loved him, still wanted to be a mother, in the end she had rejected him in favor of returning to her dazzling career. She clung to her fears instead of him and the bright future that was right there in their grasp.

Dammit! His money could buy anything. Take him and Leila anywhere they wished to go. He could ease the suffering of thousands with his charities. But his riches couldn't buy the close marriage he'd once envisioned he'd have with Leila. It couldn't buy her trust. All the wealth he'd accumulated wouldn't ensure she could have a healthy pregnancy.

Leila. She was always on his mind. A fever in his blood. Why the hell had she phoned him earlier today? Why hadn't she left a message?

The question needled him, for when he'd returned her call much later, there had been no answer. Was she all right?

He wrapped a thirsty towel around his hips and padded across the white terrazzo floor, calling himself a fool for worrying. Leila likely had a change of plans for her upcoming shoot. Perhaps she'd gotten another offer, one that would tear her away from him for another holiday, he thought sourly.

A trio of wide steps descended into his spacious living

room. He damned sure didn't want to go on like this, living apart from his wife. Virtually living alone. Putting his dream of a family with her on hold yet again while she struggled to cope with her fears and devoted more and more time to her career.

If she couldn't, or wouldn't, take a chance on them, on a family, he could be stuck in this marital limbo for years.

That prospect rested heavily on him as he drew a *bam gelado* from the bar cooler, the bottle of beer was so cold that ice coated the outside. At least this small pleasure in his life was perfect!

He opened it and drank deeply, welcoming the shock to his senses. But when the drink was finished, the quiet penthouse still felt oppressive.

Rafael cursed loud and long. He had to get out of here before the solitude drove him mad. Maybe he'd hit the clubs along Ipanema Beach tonight, see if he could connect with friends. With life.

Before he could take an impatient step toward his bedroom, the bell on his private elevator dinged. His brow furrowed in annoyance. Who had the audacity to pay him a visit without calling first? He certainly was in no mood for company.

But that was exactly what he was going to have, for his elevator was moving upward. Someone was coming. He intensely disliked surprise visitors and this time was no exception.

Hopefully it was just Nathaniel and his wife needing to crash here. If so, they could have the penthouse for as long as they wanted.

Certain that was who was paying a surprise visit, Rafael turned to the elevator with a forced smile just as the doors opened. The last person he expected to see stared back at him with huge hazel eyes, her gorgeous reflection caught in the many mirrors.

"*Leila*? What in the hell are you doing here?"

"We have to talk," she said, and stepped inside the suite, dragging a small overnight case behind her.

A blast of anger and desire erupted within him, both vying for prominence, both confirming he was far from over her. "You should have returned my call."

"I thought about it, but this was something that needed to be said face-to-face."

He didn't like her grave tone or the tension carving lines in her face. Had she, too, made a decision regarding their future? Did she want to end their marriage once and for all?

"So talk," he said, striving to be light but failing as the words came out clipped. Sharp. Cold.

She took a shaky breath. Then another.

He took an instinctive step toward her, his insides twisting with concern now. She looked pale. Tired. Terrified.

Something was very wrong.

"Very well," she said. "I'm pregnant."

CHAPTER NINE

RAFAEL prided himself on his iron control of his emotions, but that admission nearly brought him to his knees. His gaze scanned her body with exacting detail, but her loose clothes prevented him from seeing the evidence that proved her claim.

Leila was pregnant.

He'd dreamed of it. Wanted it badly. Yet the realization that she carried his child, that they would be parents, floored him.

"You are sure of this?" he asked.

"Positive. My doctor ran blood tests to confirm it," she said, eyes wide with obvious fright. "According to the doctor, I conceived in March. That's when we met in Aru—"

"I remember, *querida*."

Remembered every delicious detail of that reunion.

He swiped a hand over his mouth, sorting this out in his head. That had been the first time he'd been with his wife in eight long months and he'd been ravenous for her. Hell, they'd been starving for each other.

He gave a nervous laugh at the tremor that rocked through him. It was unbelievable. It was a dream come true.

"You are...what? Three months along?" he said, the reality of being a father in less than six months staggering him.

She nodded. "The reason I got pregnant was because I was taking an antibiotic at the same time as my pill, and it diminished the effectiveness of the birth control." Her eyes closed on a groan. "This is just such a shock. So much to cope with."

"Which you will do with me by your side now that the choice of having a child has been taken from you."

That earned him a pointed glare, but he shrugged off her annoyance at his choice of words. Call it a miracle. Fate. Everything he'd wanted was in his grasp. He wasn't about to jeopardize her health or their child's.

That meant he, too, would have to make major changes in his life. Quick decisions.

A baby changed everything, his life and hers. He hoped Leila came to realize that quickly.

He crossed to her then and wrapped her in his embrace, the towel falling to the floor forgotten. His heart soared and he longed to shout for joy, but he tempered his excitement in the face of her shock.

She was unnaturally stiff, and an occasional tremor skittered through her. He had to handle her and this situation carefully.

"Perhaps it's as you said in France," he whispered, pressing a kiss to her temple, her forehead. "Perhaps conceiving in the face of such odds was fate's choice to make."

She took a stuttering breath, her body marginally losing its unbending steel. "However it happened, it was still unplanned. Is still difficult to accept, to face my worst fears."

"We will get through this together."

He heard her swallow, felt her tension vibrate along his own taut nerves. "There's more, Rafael."

He'd never seen Leila act this serious. This worried. This terrified.

God, please don't let there be something wrong with our baby. With Leila. Give us this.

"Go on," he urged gently, his own breath held now.

She took another shaky breath and stepped back from him, though still caught in the circle of his arms. Her worried gaze lifted to his. "The ultrasound I took yesterday revealed there are two babies."

It took a moment for that to sink in. "Twins?"

She gave a wooden nod, looking as if she'd be ill any second. *Meu Deus!* She'd gone through hell trying to have one baby. How would she cope with bearing two?

For the first time he felt the sharp talons of fear scrape down his spine. Every complication he'd ever read about was now twice as dire.

"It will be all right," he said, hoping to hell that would prove true.

"Rafael, I'm terrified." She took a step backward, her eyes suddenly frantic. "I came here because…" She blinked rapidly, yet tears slipped from her eyes anyway. "I don't know what to do. I'm so afraid I'll fail us again."

He was at her side in an instant, gathering her close with hands that trembled. "Do not say that. Don't even think it. Remember that together we can do anything."

She trembled in his arms, but this time she clung to him and the fear gripping his heart eased. "You are so arrogantly sure of yourself I want to believe you."

"Never doubt I can keep you safe, *querida.*"

Since he'd seen Leila in France, he'd endlessly researched the risks attributed to recovered anorexics during pregnancy and he had a better grasp of the inner demons she battled. He had decided then that if she'd give them a chance at this, he'd make sure that not one day went past without him telling her she grew more beautiful to him. More cherished. More loved.

"I'll hire the best doctors. You will be fine," he said, con- viction in his voice that he desperately wanted to believe.

He shoved those doubts away and focused on the woman pressed to him now. His eyes closed and his throat worked.

She was his wife. Soon to be the mother to his children.

He was going to be a father. He would have Leila back as his wife. He'd have his family. He'd have everything.

"We'll relocate to the *fazenda*," he said, knowing a phone call would alert his small staff to prepare for their arrival.

"I have to return to California first."

He was shaking his head before she finished. "There is no need when you can have your things shipped here."

"I was afraid you'd do this."

She twisted out of his arms and stepped back, far enough that he'd have to take a step to reach her, enough distance to force him to realize that she'd wrestled control of her emotions.

He spread his arms wide. "I am merely doing what I promised by taking care of you and our babies."

"For now. But I know you." She lifted a hand, holding her thumb and forefinger a millimeter apart. "You are this close to turning into a tyrant."

The lightly said quip was too damned close to the horror he'd lived with all his life. His father had been a brutal auto- crat and mentally unstable thanks to an indulgence in booze and drugs.

Though Rafael had never spent a moment in the man's company, he'd lived with the fear that those dark traits would show up in him one day. For Leila to suggest such a thing, even in jest, jarred him.

He took a deep breath, then another, determined to keep a clear head. "Why would you need to fly back to California?"

"I have a doctor's appointment that I can't miss."

"There are equally qualified obstetricians in São Paulo," he said. "Since you will be living here, wouldn't it be wise to align yourself with one now?"

Leila frowned and gave the room a quick glance. Looking flustered. Or was that cornered?

She bit her lip, then huffed a breath and met his gaze. "I also have a shoot next week. My final one that wraps up this contract."

Was she crazy? "I forbid you to work now that you are pregnant!"

"You forbid me? That is not your decision to make, Rafael!" she said, her hazel eyes as hard and glittering as cut ambers now.

"The hell it isn't! These are my children you carry and you are my wife!" He raked his fingers through his hair and swore. "My God! You just came here crying, worried sick that you would do something to harm our babies. And yet you insist on working?"

She pressed her palms to her head and let out a cry of frustration. "Stop it! I've discussed the dangers of finishing this contract, and my doctor assures me that I am fine as long as I stay hydrated, am careful to rest between takes and don't take risks on the set."

"I don't like it, Leila."

"I know, but hear me out." She crossed to him slowly, eyes locked on his. He read the fear and worry and love in her gaze as she slipped her arms around him. "My agent was able to convince the designers to move the dates on the campaign so I could work without great risk at this point. Rafael, the shoot will only last a week, maybe less. I'll be close to my doctor there."

He didn't like this one bit, but all the arguing in the world was not going to change her mind. Short of locking her in a room, he couldn't hold her here.

"All right. When are you flying back to L.A.?"

"Tomorrow morning."

"Fine," he bit out, grabbing his mobile and punching in numbers. Distancing himself from her in space and emotion. "I'll go with you."

"That isn't necessary…"

He slashed the air with one hand, cutting off whatever she was about to say. "We will never be apart again, not even for a day. I won't stand on the outside and watch my family live away from me! My children will know me."

"You think I plan to stay there without you?" she asked, her brow drawn. "That I'd separate you from the children?"

He clamped his jaw tight, his cheeks burning from the memory of his youth. She didn't know all the details. Couldn't imagine the hell and shame he'd endured.

"Rafael, what's wrong? What aren't you telling me?"

He shrugged off her concern, determined to valiantly keep his shame hidden. "It's nothing."

"Yes, it is. Please. Tell me what is haunting you so," she coaxed, her hands light on his back, her breath warm on his skin. "I'm your wife. There's nothing you can't tell me. Nothing."

He hung his head, eyes pinched shut. She was right, but knowing that didn't make it any easier to unburden his soul.

"You don't know how hard this is," he said, afraid to give voice to his fears.

"Then tell me so I understand." She slipped her arms around him, and warmth seeped into him, thawing the icy dam holding his past hostage.

"You know my father disowned me," he said, his fingers digging into the window casing so hard that they went numb. "That he barred me from setting foot in Wolfe Manor."

"I remember you telling me," she said, her hands

soothing. "But your eldest brother defied him and included you with your brothers and sister."

He bobbed his head, forever grateful to Jacob for that and so much more. Jacob had done more than include him. He'd left his own inheritance for Rafael upon Rafael's eighteenth birthday.

Rafael had used it wisely, eternally grateful to his brother for giving him the opportunity to make a better life for himself and his mother. Rafael had longed to thank Jacob personally, but after William Wolfe's death Jacob had suddenly left Wolfe Manor without a word. Rafael hadn't seen his elder brother until a number of years later at a computer and technology conference in Rio.

Though he'd been unable to catch his brother that night, he'd eventually tracked him down. Their initial meeting after so many years apart had been tense at first.

But as Rafael had talked about their siblings' successes and his own rapidly expanding company, Jacob had acted like his old fun self. At least to a degree, he remembered with a frown. For Jacob had shared little of his own life.

And to Rafael's frustration, Jacob had refused to take back the fortune he'd given to Rafael so long ago. "Give it to charity," Jacob had said, sending his love on to Rafael's mother before he disappeared again.

One day he'd repay Jacob for his largess. One day…

He shook off the memory and focused on Leila again.

"Because of William Wolfe's refusal to acknowledge me or to even lend financial support, my mother was forced to work two jobs," he said, again telling her what she already knew as he eased into the subject that tormented him. "She was rarely home. Her solution to keeping me occupied and out of trouble with the wrong crowd was by supplying me with outdated computers to tinker with."

It was then that he discovered what he loved most. What

he could do better than anyone. It hadn't bothered him when he discovered those early computers were the cast-offs of his half brothers. To him they were golden opportunities to learn, to let his imagination soar.

"She obviously succeeded," Leila said.

He heaved a troubled sigh and faced her then. "She did all she could, Leila. One year she scrimped and saved so she could give me twenty pounds sterling for Christmas, but the real surprise was when she took me to London for a day so I could see the holiday finery and buy whatever I wanted."

"That's a beautiful memory," she said.

"It would have been," he said, the old pain of rejection returning full force. "Except, we walked by Hartington's, and there in the front window was a lavish Christmas display with the latest toys being enjoyed by my brothers and sister."

"Your father's store."

He managed a curt nod, seeing it all unfold as if it were yesterday. The cold. The pristine sprinkling of snow.

The family he longed to be part of together. Happy.

Just like then, the pain of rejection and hatred sliced through him with the precision of a honed blade, leaving him emotionally bleeding.

"My father was there as well, standing to the side of the display, watching his children perform for the crowds gathered outside." He swallowed hard, but the bitter memory lingered on his tongue, the despondency and wretched exclusion that engulfed him then was still almost unbearable. "When he saw me and my mother standing there in the cold and snow, his eyes glittered with hatred while his hard mouth twisted into a cruel smile."

Leila let out a cry of despair. "How could a father treat his child so abominably?"

It was a question that Rafael had asked himself thousands of times but could never answer. His father had been a victim to violent mood swings egged on by drink and later drugs, he'd discovered.

That realization kept Rafael from envying his siblings for what they had, for they had to suffer their father's wrath daily. When Jacob passed his inheritance down to Rafael, his mother had bought him the best computer on the market.

And in two months he'd channeled all his past hurt and shame into a wildly creative endeavor and reprogrammed his old computer to make it even better.

There had been no stopping him from achieving what he wanted from then on.

There wouldn't be now either.

He turned and cupped her narrow shoulders, staring down into her worried face and thinking he was the luckiest man on earth to have found her. "That is why I refuse to be an absentee father, or allow us to live apart."

"Oh, Rafael! Can't you see you are nothing like that man?"

"For now. But, Leila, if those horrid traits ever emerge in me, promise me you will pack up our babies and leave me. Get as far from me as you can and don't look back."

Her face bleached of color, like driftwood left too long on a sun-baked beach. "I can't do—"

"Promise me!"

One tear slipped from her wide eyes, then another. "I promise. But I know it will *never* come to that."

He managed a stage smile, wishing he had just an ounce of her confidence.

CHAPTER TEN

W<small>HILE</small> Leila slept during the flight back to Los Angeles, Rafael tended to business. Delegating was not something he did willingly or often, yet this time he had no choice.

He had made the decision to be with Leila this week, even though he had a crucial meeting planned. His family came first now.

With a few keystrokes, he'd placed his next in command in charge of the meeting. The next hour had been spent sending accompanying documents for the meeting with a lengthy letter detailing Rafael's stand on the next big step the company was to take.

He'd never left such a monumental decision in an employee's hands before. He damned sure wasn't comfortable doing so now.

But a greater risk was at stake here.

His wife. His children. *His family!*

He was ever mindful that Leila had gone through part of this before. Alone.

Try as he might, he couldn't forget the grief in her eyes when she spoke of losing their first baby. Of her very real fears now. She'd taken the knife of trust and sliced open an emotional vein, bleeding onto his heart, his soul.

He couldn't fail her. Fail them.

Rafael closed the browser on his PDA and exhaled heavily.

He was certain Leila had been honest with him. That she held no more secrets. No more demons.

If only he could say the same!

He'd yet to tell her the whole truth surrounding his birth. A fact he'd learned at the tender age of eight when cruel villagers had revealed his mother's dark secret—that William Wolfe had paid her to have sex with him.

He'd not been entirely sure what that had meant at the time. When he'd asked his mother, she'd flushed and told him to forget about it, but he'd not been able to.

In time he learned what being paid to sleep with a man signified. A painfully demoralizing lesson that he'd never forgotten. That had left him hating his mother for nearly a year. Hating her nearly as much as he hated the brutally cruel William Wolfe!

Yet you learned to trust your mother again, to understand her reasoning. To be proud of her for doing what she had to do, knowing it would mark her for life.

And what of Leila? She had deceived him by keeping her miscarriage secret. Yet his conscience was quick to remind him that he was just as much at fault for leaving her alone.

He drew in a slow deep breath and then expelled his pent-up tension in one long shuttering exhalation. The lack of sleep and emotional stress were playing hell with his mind.

He glanced at the woman softly dozing beside him and felt his heart warm even as his gut clenched with concern. If he lost her and their babies, he'd never forgive himself.

Leila's mobile began singing a haunting melody by a popular Celtic singer that disrupted the silence. Even though he found the music appealing, he was annoyed that the call would rob her of much-needed sleep.

Mouthing a curse, he followed the direction of the music to find her mobile was quite visible in her open bag beside her chair. He didn't hesitate to reach down to mute it. But he hadn't realized that in grabbing her phone, he'd pulled out a scrap of paper too.

With her phone now silent and returned to her bag, he retrieved the note that had dropped on the floor. A clinic's name was jotted on it with a Canadian address.

He certainly didn't recognize the place. Yet the hair on his nape stood on end just the same.

She had a Californian doctor. Why would she need one in Canada as well? Was there another shoot planned there that she'd neglected to tell him about?

In a matter of seconds, he'd tapped the clinic's name into his web browser. Two things happened at once.

The jet hit a pocket of air and dropped a jarring degree in altitude, waking Leila with a startled cry. And his browser window opened to reveal that the clinic was one that specialized in abortion.

A red cloud of rage drifted over him.

Had her paralyzing fear and grief convinced her that this was a possibility? Had she considered ridding herself of their babies?

"I hope we're nearly there," Leila said, oblivious to his darkening mood.

He cut her a sharp look and had the satisfaction of seeing her flinch. "Why are you carrying around the name of an abortion clinic? Were you thinking of doing this vile thing?"

Her mouth worked, but the only sound that came out was a sputtering moan that was too high-pitched and too shaky. "My agent gave me the name of that clinic in case I wanted to pursue that option. I'd forgotten I even had it."

It galled him that she'd sought her agent's advice when she should have come to him immediately! Okay, so she had come to him in the end. But what if she hadn't? What if she'd been pressured into doing the unthinkable because of her damn career?

He remembered well what she'd told him of her first rise to fame in modeling. That when her waif image began changing as she matured her mother and agent had taught her how to control her meals to the extreme. How she had often binged on food as she had been so hungry, before purging herself and then starving herself for days. How they had both nearly killed her.

"Did you even consider this?" he asked.

She reeled back as if he had slapped her. "That you would ask such a question proves you don't know me at all!"

He stiffened, ready to argue that he did know her. And in that split second he saw a distorted image of himself, railing like a crazed man consumed with rage. *Like his father?*

The comparison was sobering. Chilling. He was shamed at his own actions.

"The greater question to ask is why is that note in your hands?" Leila asked. "Did you search my purse? Do you distrust me that much that you have to look through my possessions as if I were a rebellious teenager?"

"The note fell on the floor when I pulled your phone out to silence it."

She simply stared at him, as if expecting more.

He swore, not at her but at himself. "I'm sorry, *querida.*"

Her shoulders bowed, and she almost seemed to cave in on herself. Before he could reach out to support her, she stiffened in her seat.

"After all I've told you about losing our first baby, how could you think for one moment that I'd do something like that?" she asked.

This was the steel he'd recognized in Leila from the moment he'd met her. A core of strength that hinted at a young woman who had escaped her humble beginnings and had seen more than she should have seen. Who'd been scarred by her past, much like he'd been emotionally scarred.

Yet he, in his arrogance and shock, had lashed out first. All his old doubts and fears that he'd become a monster reared its head. Yet he refused to give them breath. Refused to allow that fear to suffocate him again.

He reached over and cupped Leila's silken cheek, and breathed a sigh of relief when she didn't pull away from him. "I only wanted you to rest, *querida*."

"You have a strange way of showing concern."

For a moment he thought she'd say more, but she shook her head and closed her eyes, shutting him out as securely as if she'd slammed a door in his face. His face burned, as did his conscience.

Everything he'd ever wanted had been placed before him now. Yet here he was, being an overbearing, arrogant ass, interrogating her over an address he'd found in her purse. Assuming the worst of her instead of trusting her.

"I had to know the truth," he said.

Again she didn't reply. Didn't so much as look his way.

He swore, not waiting for his jet to taxi to a stop before ripping off his seat belt. So far he'd handled this very badly.

He knelt beside her chair and took her stiff hands in his, his gut clenching as she trembled. "Don't shut me out, *querida*."

She shook her head and he caught the telling quiver of her lower lip. "I don't want to, Rafael, but when you act so strong and dominant, I instinctively rebel against you. You cannot control me, Rafael."

He downed his head and sighed, for her pregnancy seemed to bringing out the worst in him. It shamed him. Enraged him to be this way with her.

"I only want to protect you and our babies. It is clear I

failed you before," he said, well aware he needed to calm the storm brewing in her soul. "I won't fail you again. Tomorrow you will go to your shoot and I will escort you to the location and will simply be a quiet observer. No control."

She cast him a wary look. "Okay."

Okay. That was a start.

In moments, he hailed a cab to take them to her residence. And he was quickly hit with another surprise to learn that she no longer lived in the mansion in Brentwood.

When they'd met, she'd just bought the massive house. He'd seen it once and thought it garish in the extreme, but her mother had adored it and had deemed it her residence.

"When did you move?" he asked as he caught a glimpse of the low, squat house the moment the limo passed through the security gate.

"Seven months ago," she said as the taxi pulled up in front of the house that nestled back in the woods, nearly hidden.

He frowned. That would have been shortly before her miscarriage.

"Why didn't you tell me you'd moved?" he asked.

"Perhaps for the same reason you never told me you now owned a farm in São Paulo," she said, and then with a shrug, added, "You were away then, and by the time you returned..." She shook her head and stared out the window.

By then she'd lost their child. Recovered. And had dived right back into her career.

Her house was a blend of Spanish and American architecture and instantly reminded him of his *casa*. She would like their *fazenda*, he thought as he followed her inside. She would make it a home.

The salon was alive with color and heavy black ironwork, more of an old California than Spanish flavor. The land was thickly forested hills, broken by large grassy fields.

The concern that needled him earlier doubled. From the large expanse of glass, the view of the ocean was spectacular, but the house was fairly remote with only the occasional rooftop of neighbors tucked into the hillside marring the vista.

"Do you have guards?"

She laughed, as if the idea was ludicrous. "Electronic ones. The house and grounds are equipped with a state-of-the-art security system. It can detect when anyone breeches the perimeter."

Not always. Even sophisticated systems like this could be overridden by a clever hacker.

"A gated community would be safer."

She cut him a dubious look. "Because we all can be sure that our neighbor is the trustworthy sort?" Before he could respond to that, she snorted and went on. "I don't want to live that way, Rafael. I never did. Being that close to neighbors reminds me of the *favelas*. There was no privacy. No security. Everyone knew everyone's business there."

He nodded in understanding, for while he'd grown up in a small flat, there had been no secrets in the village. Which is why he preferred his hacienda carved out of the rain forest. It was a compound with an adequate staff who knew how to make themselves blend into their surroundings.

There he felt free.

And once Leila moved in with him, once their children were born, he'd no longer feel so alone, so adrift in this world.

"Are you hungry?" she asked, dropping her bag on the terrazzo floor and striding into the kitchen, her heels tapping out a beat that matched the pounding of his heart.

"Ravenous," he said, the sway of her hips leaving him carnally aching for her.

He ruthlessly tamped down that desire and joined her in a kitchen that was light and airy. After reading about the dangers Leila could face, he wouldn't make love to her until he'd spoken with a doctor. Even then he wasn't sure that *he* was willing to take that risk just to satisfy his lust.

"Where would you like to eat?" he asked, kicking himself for not insisting they stop at a restaurant before they got to her house. But then he hadn't known she'd moved out into the hills. He hadn't guessed she didn't have a housekeeper or cook on staff.

"Right here."

Leila? Cook? She surprised him by preparing huge salads teeming with fresh vegetables, ripe cheeses and a blend of native olives. For his benefit, she added steamed chicken and a crisp Californian chardonnay.

He carried the food out onto the patio that overlooked the cliffs, marveling at how domestic she clearly was. He hadn't known that about her, but then they had spent a year apart. The meal was light, the warm breeze refreshing and the view of the glowing orange sun dipping into the sea breathtaking.

Yet he found himself more content to watch her. To just be in her company and share this quiet time with her.

And it was quiet. Isolated. How long would it take her to get medical help from here? Who'd know if she needed help if she was here alone?

"I would like to visit your doctor," he said.

Her brow narrowed the slightest bit, and for a moment he was sure she'd argue.

"I have an appointment tomorrow after the session. You're welcome to come along."

As if he needed an invitation!

"How long does it take you to reach your doctor or the hospital?" he asked.

"If the traffic is moving, I can get there in forty-five minutes."

"That's too long in an emergency," he said, his insides clenching at how much precious time would be wasted to get her to a hospital. "It is less than twenty minutes from the *fazenda* to the highest-rated obstetrician and hospital in all of Brazil."

"You've researched every aspect of this already?"

He gave a brief nod, for once he realized the risks she faced, he couldn't stop until he'd left no stone unturned. "I want the best for you and our babies."

"You want me under your control in Brazil."

"I want you safe," he reiterated, the ringing of her mobile an irritation he could have lived without.

While he would have preferred she let it ring, she pushed her half-eaten salad aside and took the call. "Yes, I know the place. Is the second session there as well?"

Second session? When had this come about?

"Okay," she said. "It's better to get it all done in one day if possible. Thanks for the update."

"I gather that was your agent," he said, rocking back in his chair to savor his wine after she ended the call.

"Yes, she always gives me a courtesy call before a session, especially if there has been a change." She tried to stifle a yawn and failed. "The photographer wants to do both sessions tomorrow because he won't be back in L.A. for six weeks. By then I will be showing."

By then Rafael hoped for them to be settled into their home in São Paulo. But he resisted bringing that topic up now.

She got to her feet and yawned again. "Two flights so

close together have exhausted me, so forgive me for seeking bed so soon."

He waved aside her apology, more concerned that she was this weary. Was that normal? Should she call her doctor? Should he?

His mobile vibrated in his pocket, and he frowned, annoyed that someone had chosen that moment to ring him. He spared a moment to check the display and swore. His manager wouldn't ring him unless it was urgent.

"Sorry, I can't ignore this," he said to Leila, looking up with an apologetic frown. But she had already gone inside the house, leaving him alone with his worries and his hopes rattling through him.

The rest of the evening was lost for him in business, long phone calls and even longer hours poring over designs on his laptop. By the time he'd finished it was after midnight. His back ached and his head swam with numbers and codes, none of it making sense to him any longer.

The house was dark. Quiet.

He found the bedroom, stripped off his clothes and crawled into bed beside her, pulling her into the curve of his body. His palm splayed over her flat belly.

She moaned in her sleep and snuggled closer. He smiled, his heart full, but worry quickly intruded.

His wife. His babies. He'd never forgive himself if he failed to keep them safe.

That mantra whispered through him the following morning as he drove Leila to the session, the powerful car maneuvering the winding coastal highway with ease. The site of the shoot along the jagged rocks that spilled into the ocean was breathtaking and hinted of danger.

The photographer applauded her professionalism and Rafael appreciated his wife's poise and beauty against a backdrop of stone and sand and sea. She made her job look effortless when he knew it was demanding.

However, the afternoon session farther up the coast in a small seaside town was entirely different, all because by the time the light was right, Leila's sizzling energy was fading. While her body was perfect and her smile captivating, there was a remoteness in her eyes.

"Just a couple more, Leila," the photographer said after she'd taken a break to refresh her makeup and hydrate herself. "Work with me. Let's do this right in one so we can get out of here."

Leila shook her arms, stretched, then struck a pose that was pure seduction. His entire body hummed with want of her.

"That's it," the photographer said, rapidly snapping shots and shifting his position to capture her in a variety of angles. "Now go for the kill."

Rafael made to step back. But her gaze swung to his and locked. Hot. Glittering with challenge and sensual promise.

His mouth went dry as blood surged through him in hot urgent pulses. His sex grew heavy and stiff. Just like at the shoots in the south of France.

But unlike then, he quickly got caught up in this new dangerous game. An alarmingly public game.

It was the first time he'd let down the walls of his own control where anyone but Leila could see him. But nobody was watching him. Just her.

And right now her smoldering eyes were blazing into his.

He paced, stoking the fires of her passion with his eyes, tossing more kindling on his own. *I want you naked and under me,* querida!

She lifted her chin, quick to join him in this visual foreplay, tracking him with her eyes. As if challenging him to take her now!

There was something deeply erotic in standing in the shadows with her under the spotlight making love to him with her eyes. Of knowing everyone in the room was watching her. Aroused by her expressions, her seductive poses.

"That's it," the photographer said, rapidly snapping pictures. "Move with it, Leila. Come on, sweetheart, pour it on."

And she did just that, her hot gaze stroking every inch of Rafael until he thought he'd go up in flames. Surely his eyes smoldered with passion as they caressed the full swell of her upthrust breasts and the nipples that had hardened in want of his fingers and lips.

He ached to move with the provocative sway of her hips. To feel the press of her tight round bottom against his erection and stroke the sweet silken flesh between her thighs that would be wet and ready for him now.

By the time the photographer gave a satisfied nod and ended the session, Rafael was in agony with his unquenched desire. Leila looked ready to rip off her clothes and seduce him then and there.

But when he escorted her to the passenger door of her car, he heard her wince. "What's wrong?"

She eased onto the seat, her eyes seeming too huge, her face too flushed. But it was the hand pressed to her stomach that sent a chill streaking down his spine.

"I had a sharp pain in my side just then," she said. "I must have stayed in one position too long on the set."

Though it was possible she was right, his concern that this could be the start of a more dangerous issue stormed through his mind. But saying that would alarm her, and that was exactly what he wanted to avoid.

He slammed behind the wheel and took off down the

highway toward L.A. as fast as he dared. "Call your doctor and see if he wants you to come to his office, or go to the hospital."

"I'm sure you are overreacting," she said, but she was making the call while she spoke.

Impatience crashed through him in cold icy waves as he listened to her explain her pain to whoever answered the phone. "I don't think so. No, just the one time. Okay, we are on our way."

"Where?" he asked, forcing his voice to remain calm when he was far from calm.

"The doctor's office," she said, and gave him directions.

Due to a traffic snarl, the hour and a half drive took close to two hours. Rafael's nerves stretched to the breaking point and snapped.

He careered into a parking slot and slammed on the brakes, his blood as hot as the powerful engine. "It takes far too long to get from one point to another in this city."

"The traffic can be unpredictable," she said, her features tight, not with pain but concern.

He took her hand, entwining his fingers with hers, his heart skipping a beat as her tremors passed through him. "I know you trust your doctor, but I will rest easier when you are back in our home in São Paulo."

Again she nodded, and he sensed before she spoke that she wouldn't balk, that today's snarl on the freeway had proved his point. "Yes, so will I."

He finally drew a decent breath, then lifted their joined hands to place a warm kiss on the back of her smooth flawless skin. "Good. Let's see this doctor now."

After the doctor examined Leila, he ordered an abdominal ultrasound. Hearing his babies' hearts beat, seeing them move inside Leila, was a joy that was beyond anything Rafael had experienced. His emotions were so overwhelming that he was glad the room was dark and nobody asked him to speak.

"You suffered mild heat cramps caused by too much sun and a strenuous workday," the doctor said later. "I'd recommend you cut back on your work, Leila."

"I am," she said, and Rafael heaved another sigh of relief.

He thanked the doctor and took Leila's hand, loving her more than words could say. "Let's go home, *querida*."

CHAPTER ELEVEN

IN THEIR five years of marriage they'd called only two places home. The first apartment they'd shared in Rio, and later the penthouse.

They'd always lived in the midst of excitement. The bustling life of Rio or the exciting nightlife along the coast.

But as Rafael's private jet landed some hours later in Ribeirão Preto, she admitted she looked forward to the change of pace. A limo was waiting to take them from the airport.

Though she was tired, her gaze devoured the beauty of the farmland. Many of the red fields lay bare, or riddled with stubble. But the fields of sugarcane teemed with workers harvesting the crop.

This life was vastly different than what either of them had known. Though he'd always talked of buying land one day, she'd never wondered why until now.

"What made you want to live out here?" she asked.

He took a deep breath and smiled. "I can breathe out here. Relax."

She nodded, finding it refreshing that they shared this. "I felt the same way about Malibu."

"You'll like it here."

And she did.

The *casa* was fabulous, though not nearly as large as

she'd expected a billionaire would own. Another surprise was the house staff, which was small, almost invisible.

He gave her a brief tour of the *casa*, pride ringing in his voice. Though she could see the historical dignity of the old coffee plantation had been kept intact, his office was as he'd told her—the ultimate in high-tech.

As for the bedroom they would share, it was simply sumptuous. But it was obvious he hadn't spent much time here. The closets and dresser were nearly empty!

Just staring at that void was a shock, for no matter where she'd lived, she was surrounded by a vast array of clothes, most supplied by the various companies she'd worked for. Always more than she'd ever need, which was why she auctioned the majority of them to help her clinic in São Paulo.

And secretly, there was another reason she felt at ease when faced with the latest wardrobe she was to model. They were all the same size—the size she was to maintain. How would she cope with a closet full of maternity clothes, all designed to accommodate her increasing abdomen? Who'd know if she gained extra pounds, or lost them?

Don't think that way!

She wouldn't let the past ruin her future. The doctor had given her a chart that listed what weight she should safely gain during her pregnancy. As long as she stayed within those parameters, she'd be okay. She *had* to be okay!

But there was still the worry over how to spend her days. Though Rafael had promised to spend the bulk of his time here, she knew that he'd still have to put in long hours working.

She'd be alone in an area where she knew nobody. Where she had nothing to do but think. For someone with her past history, that could be a dangerous thing. More dangerous than if she worked.

So what was she going to do for the next six months? How could she keep from going stir-crazy?

She crossed to the window and took in the old plantation from a new angle. She had expected a highly efficient compound, and Rafael's *fazenda* was that and more, right down to the small army of men in the fields.

"Do the workers live here or in town?"

"Most live in the dormitory I built for them." He pointed to a fairly large building off to the right.

She frowned, for it didn't look near large enough to house the workers plus their families. Surely Rafael wasn't exploiting the poor, not after producing a film that cut right to the heart of Rio's poverty issues.

"Isn't that terribly crowded for families?" she asked.

"The few families that I employ have their own cottages," he said. "The field laborers that you see are young men from the Rio slums."

She blinked, not expecting that. She looked from them to him. "All of them?"

He nodded. "I met most of these boys over a year ago when I visited the *favelas*, gathering research for our film. Some came from fractured homes, with a parent either disabled or dead from the gang wars. Most were homeless."

How well she knew that life! How desperately she'd wanted to escape it after her father's and brother's deaths.

"All of these boys were extremely eager to work for us then." Rafael frowned, as if troubled by a memory. "When the project was over, I couldn't just walk away from them."

The apprehension that had seized her lost its grip in one long exhalation. "So you gave them jobs."

"Yes, but I also gave them the chance to better their lives if they wished. Each boy is given the opportunity to take classes," he said simply. "If they have an education or steady job, they are less likely to return to the gangs."

She stared at the young men again until tears stung her eyes. They all looked healthy. Happy.

At that moment, she loved Rafael more than she thought possible. Though he was austere and often demanding on the surface, deep inside beat the heart of a very compassionate man.

Though she was proud of the clinic she'd established to help the poor girls of São Paulo afflicted with the same disease she'd battled, his work far outshined her efforts. For he was not only saving lives, he was saving the future of Brazil.

If only an opportunity like this had been offered her father and brother...

To her surprise sudden tears filled her eyes. She blinked, trying to hold them back. But the effort was futile.

"*Querida*, what's wrong?" he asked, pulling her against his chest.

She shook her head, hating to tell him a lie. Yet how could she open the door on the past she had locked away? How could she expect him to understand why she'd never been able to tell him about the horrible event that changed her life forever?

He gripped her arms and held her from him, his gaze boring into her, his features taut with worry. "Leila, you are scaring me. What is it that's troubling you?"

She bit back a watery laugh born of nerves, her hands finally finding purchase on his incredibly broad chest. She splayed them over hard muscle and warm flesh, letting his heat seep into her and thaw her choking fears.

"Everything that you depicted in the film *Carnival*, I lived through to one degree or another. Everything," she emphasized, hoping he'd understand that she had seen every vile thing one person could do to another at a young age, that she, too, had lived in that poverty-ridden war zone.

Rafael cared for the desperately poor. The way he managed his farm and provided for the boys he'd rescued from the slums proved that to her.

"There were no saviors like you in the *favelas* when I was a child. If there had been, perhaps my father would still be alive. Perhaps my brother would too, and have his own family and home because of the largess of someone like y—"

He pressed a finger over her lips, silencing her. "There is still much to do. You and I have the chance to make a difference for our people. That is a good thing, *querida*."

The tears she'd thought were spent stung her eyes. "We could work together on this?"

"If you wish, though I understand how much you need to control your clinic."

Fire streaked across her cheeks. How stupid she'd been to think her efforts would have gotten lost under his corporate umbrella. But then she hadn't realized his own work among the desperately poor was this extensive.

"I love you," she said.

"And you are my heart as well." He bent and kissed her tear-streaked eyes, her nose that was surely red, her lips that were raw from her nervously biting them. "Rest. I'll call you when dinner is served."

She nodded again and reluctantly pulled from his arms. The bed was monstrous. Yet she crawled on it and curled on her side, intending to rest a few minutes. The worst was over.

Or was it? she wondered, her hands sliding protectively to her stomach.

Leila woke an hour later, much rested. And ravenous! The enticing aroma drifting down the hallway only increased her appetite. When had she eaten last?

Perhaps she could beg a snack from the cook…

The thought fizzled like cola on her tongue as she stepped into the bright airy kitchen and her gaze lit on the handsome man standing at the stove. He wore snug jeans that hugged his lean hips and long legs, and a white T-shirt that emphasized his broad muscular back and golden skin.

A skillet sizzled before him and a spicy aroma escaped a pot of beans and rice, the enticing smells drifting on the warm air.

"I'm impressed," she said, coming closer. "And very grateful you're fixing what I hope is our dinner."

"*Feijoada*. My mother used to cook it when I was a boy. Coming home always makes me hunger for it." His dark eyes flicked over her. "Much like I hunger for you, *querida*."

"It's safe to say you have an unquenchable appetite," she said in a teasing tone, hiding the worry that clung deep inside her. Would his hunger for her still be as consuming once she began to grow? Would he still be as attentive?

Stop thinking that your worth is equated with your weight! But right now the old fears were playing hell with her hormones, a thing her doctor had warned her about.

"I hope you have fresh vegetables too," she said, breaking the intense gaze of his by moving to the refrigerator.

"Always," he said. "I suspected you would turn up your nose at Brazilian comfort foods in favor of a salad."

She hadn't used to, but it seemed a lifetime ago when she had been a child as thin as a string bean and able to eat anything without putting on a gram. But once she'd turned that corner into adulthood and had begun to gain weight, she had learned to acquire a taste for fresh vegetables seasoned with the lightest dash of olive oil and enhanced with herbs.

"How is your mother?" she asked as she placed an array

of vegetables on the island counter and began making a salad, smoothly switching the subject, and her thoughts, from her eating habits.

"She is well. Busy," he added with a frown. "She manages a day care center in her village which commands all her time."

Did she hear a note of resentment in his tone? "That's admirable."

He gave a halfhearted shrug. "It's unnecessary! I have provided well for her. She doesn't need to hold a job."

She wasn't sure whether to pity him for feeling abandoned by his mother or angry with him for being so dictatorial. "Have you ever thought that she takes pleasure working with children? That she feels good about herself when she stays busy?"

"Exactly what she claims," he said with no small degree of annoyance.

"Tell me, Rafael. Are you opposed to the majority of women working or just your mother and wife?"

He cut her a sharp look, then turned his attention back to monitoring his meal which was far more tempting than her fresh vegetables. Like the man?

"My mother is of an age where she should be enjoying her life. Traveling. Taking it easy," he said with an arrogant lift of his chin. "As for you, you know how I feel about you working once the babies are here."

"Actually, I think something else troubles you deeply than the mere thought of me working. What it is I can't imagine."

He crossed to her in three angry steps and cupped her chin, forcing her to look into his dark eyes that snapped with annoyance and a deep and troubled glint that made her heart ache, made her breath catch and a shiver pass over her.

"You want to know what concerns me about you

returning to your career after the babies are born?" he bit out, heat blazing in his voice. "Fine! I'll tell you. I know you, *querida*. You are obsessed with every aspect of your career."

"I am a perfectionist," she clarified, jerking free of his grasp and the accusation she didn't want to face.

That earned her a derisive snort. "You won't be able to simply work an occasional session. One shoot will turn into three. Before long, you will be jaunting around the world again on campaigns." His eyes blazed into hers. "Who will care for our children then?"

She hiked up her chin, but her bravado just as quickly fizzled. "I will, with the help of a nurse or nanny."

He flung a hand upward and cursed. "You would leave our children in the care of a stranger so you could return to your career?"

"No! I'd take them and the nanny with me—"

"Like hell!"

There was anger and something else she could not identify in his expression. But its raw intensity startled her. Touched something in her that defused the last of her anger.

He raked a hand through his hair. "The children will live in their home. I won't have you drag them around the world."

She wasn't about to argue, for he was right. She did have control issues to deal with. And though she flung out that scenario, she wouldn't want to tear her children away from their home. To leave them subjected to the paparazzi while a session wore on and on.

"Okay. Point made," she said, conceding that easily.

He gave a clipped nod, still oddly tense. Had she touched on something else that troubled him? Something that he didn't want to face?

"I'm glad we are in agreement," he said.

"We aren't." She held her ground as his head snapped up, dark eyes locking on hers again. "I won't argue that the children are better off staying here with me for the most part. But know this. I'm cutting back on my career, but I'm not giving it up."

He planted both hands on his hips when she suspected he was tempted to drive them through a wall.

She took in his challenging posture and carefully blanked expression and knew he'd shut her out. Knew she'd have to cut to the heart of what troubled him before they could resolve this battle. And though they'd kept their voices tempered for the most part, it was clearly a battle of wills.

Leila affected a sweet smile that had him scowling even more. "While *I* am working, I thought you could watch our children those few times I'm away. After all, they deserve to know both of their parents."

"The children will know me. I will spend much of my time here," he said.

"Yes, working."

"I will make time to be with them."

"How good of you," she said, knowing that she'd touched on an issue that troubled him deeply. "Rafael, all you have talked about since we met was having a family. You say you don't want me to work, you want me to stay home and be with the children. Yet you plan to continue with your career and *make time* for your children. Is that the kind of family you want?"

Rafael didn't respond. In fact, he didn't say a word as he took plates from a cabinet and turned back to the stove.

Leila huffed out a weary sigh. When the subject got too personal, he retreated into his shell. Right now that broad back was racked tight with tension while he focused all his attention on cooking, using it as his shield to stop her from prying beyond the tiny bit he was willing to reveal.

It was almost as if he were afraid to be responsible for his own children! As soon as that thought crossed her mind, she knew what troubled Rafael. Her proud, strong husband was afraid to be *alone* with his children. To be responsible for them. That's why he wanted her to be at home all the time, so he wouldn't have to care for his children without her. And she knew exactly who to blame.

My God, such emotional scars that beast of a man had left on the son he refused to claim!

Rafael placed a generous portion of barbecued meat on a plate and passed it to her. She took it automatically, willing him to open up to her. But he didn't say a word as he prepared a plate for himself.

Leila set her meal on the table and dropped onto a chair. Though the intense aroma was so enticing she nearly drooled, her stomach was so tied in knots she doubted she would be able to swallow a bite.

"You're not like him, Rafael," she said when he finally joined her, every inch of his gorgeously honed frame taut with glacial tension. "You'll be a good father."

"You don't know that." The uncertainty in her brave husband's voice terrified her.

She reached over and ran her palm over his corded arm, feeling the tight coil of tension that held him stiff. "I know you are gentle. Kind. Loving. Our children will adore you, and you'll spoil them rotten."

He downed his head, breathing hard, taking it all in but saying nothing. She bit her lower lip, more concerned about his fears than her own right now. And that's what had him in its grip. Fear that he would be like his father. That he might harm their children.

That was an emotion she understood far too well, she

thought as she stared at her plate. She'd barely touched a bite, but then their conversation had pretty much killed her appetite.

"I need your help, Rafael." That brought his gaze up to hers, and she cringed at the inner pain reflected in those dark troubled eyes. "I'm afraid that as I grow, I won't be able to cope with the changes. That I'll skip meals. Lose weight."

"What do you want me to do?"

"Watch over me," she said. "Help me turn into the mother I want to be, and I'll do all I can to prove to you that you're a far better man, and father, than your own ever could be."

He stared at her for the longest time. Finally, he turned his hand over, the palm up in a silent plea that tugged at her heart.

"All right," he said.

Leila swallowed the well of emotion clogging her throat and reached over, resting her hand in his. His long fingers clasped hers, not tight, but she felt the intense connection clear to her soul.

A ghost of a smile touched his mouth, and the tension that pounded through her started to lessen. But they still had a mountain to climb.

Her gaze lowered to their joined hands again. This was the invisible thread that bound them together. Fragile. Tenuous.

It wouldn't take much to break it. To shatter them as well. Could two damaged souls mend the wounds of their pasts?

She hoped so, for it wasn't just about them anymore. Two precious lives depended on both of them to triumph.

Much like they'd done at the film festival in France, they fell into a lazy routine that carried them through the next few weeks. She became familiar with the small house staff, immediately liking the housekeeper and cook. She learned that the gardener was from the same small village as her mother.

She and Rafael had also visited with a noted obstetrician in São Paulo. Though much of her initial fears had been eliminated at that first visit, she was still guarded about her pregnancy and her own ability to accept the inevitable changes in her body.

The days passed with her and Rafael lounging on the patio taking in the sun, watching a film together in his home theater and strolling in the garden hand in hand. Neither spoke of their fears.

She told how she'd like to decorate the nursery, hoping to get his feedback as well. His reply was that she could buy whatever she needed and hire as many as it took to get the work done. As if she didn't have the funds to do what she wished.

At night they slept in each other's arms, holding on tight as if afraid this would suddenly end. The doctor had even told them that lovemaking was fine as long as they didn't do anything too physical. But Rafael still hadn't made a move to seduce her, and she'd been so afraid he'd rebuff her that she'd not attempted any seduction.

It was those little things that needled her more and more, making her feel as if she were just another of his possessions. As if all she'd said to him that day was for naught.

She almost looked forward to the hours he was called in to his office in Rio on urgent business, an event that was occurring much more often.

Leila knew that before long Rafael would be consumed with his company again, that she'd be alone here in this beautiful hacienda, growing fat with her babies and more uncertain of what the future would hold for her career, and her marriage. And with her state of mind, for as her body began to distort, she found herself growing more and more restless.

One month after her return to Brazil, Rafael excused himself to attend to business after lunch, leaving her to enjoy the serenity of the beautifully tended garden alone. But this time one hour turned into three.

While she knew that he was indeed worried about a glitch in his new hardware that his techs had yet to perfect, a tiny voice in her head used this solitude to feed her deepest fears.

He had to have noticed the drastic changes in her body just this week. Breasts that were fuller, the nipples supersensitized to his lightest touch. The baby bump had altered her perfectly toned body into something she'd never dreamed she'd see.

Her hands slid over the sun-warmed dress covering her belly, the increased roundness a shock that sometimes threatened to erupt into panic. She had to focus on the fact she was pregnant with twins. That the changes were normal and were to be cherished.

But it was hard to toss off the old neurosis of an eating disorder. If she had something to do besides read or watch the TV.

Frustrated and far too emotional of late, Leila swung her long tanned legs off the chaise longue and cradled her face in her hands. She'd been able to cope with having nothing to do as long as Rafael was around. Now that his company was tugging him from her, the isolation was driving her crazy.

She loosed a perturbed groan and surged to her feet. Perhaps a walk in the garden would expend some of the restless energy building inside her.

Before she'd taken two steps toward the pebbled path,

her mobile rang. She stared at the phone, the sound almost foreign to her ears as her agent hadn't called since she'd taken a maternity hiatus.

"Hello," Leila said in greeting, giddily delighted that she hadn't been totally forgotten.

"How are you feeling now?" her agent inquired.

"Wonderful." Unless she counted anxious and worried about far too many things that were out of her control. "The morning sickness is a thing of the past," she added, along with her formerly honed figure.

"Good! Are you ready to work, then?"

Leila blinked, not sure she heard her right. "I thought— God, yes!"

Her agent laughed, and in an instant a good deal of Leila's anxiety fell away. "First off, how much are you showing?"

"It's very obvious I'm pregnant."

"Excellent," her agent said, stunning her. "You've been offered a fabulous opportunity. *Fit Pregnancy* wants you to grace their cover, and I have another publication on the verge of offering for you as well. Interested?"

She danced around in a circle, literally giddy with relief. "Of course I am! Please, tell me more."

Her agent explained the allure of celebrity pregnancies in exacting detail. The first magazine wanted her to grant an interview and they wanted it right now. The second was a small spread for a major designer of maternity wear that likely wouldn't occur until next month or later.

"When word got out that you'd taken maternity leave, the offers started coming in," her agent explained. "These two are the most lucrative and will not be intrusive on your privacy. Both will do wonders at keeping your name out there."

Leila wiped the tears of joy from her eyes and laughed,

feeling more energized than she had in weeks. "When do I start?"

"Tomorrow, if possible. I'll send the contract to you via courier today."

"Great! I'll sign and return them to you immediately."

She clutched the phone, eyes pinched shut and smiling like a fool.

"Good news?" Rafael asked in a tight voice that set off alarms in her head.

She whirled to face him, wondering how much he'd overheard. His expression gave nothing away, but the deep creases fanning from his dark unreadable eyes didn't imbue confidence either.

Considering his earlier stance regarding her career, he'd not see this as good fortune. In fact, he'd likely see it as traitorous since she'd been sure that the shoot in L.A. was the last she'd do until well after she'd given birth.

"It's fabulous news," she said, willing her former assurance to assert itself in the face of the anger sure to come. "I've been offered a contract for a leading magazine with another in the offing."

"I trust you refused."

"I accepted."

His handsome features pulled into a fierce expression that made a chill slip down her spine. "I forbid it!"

She shoved caution aside and hiked her chin up in a show of defiance. "You can't order me around! This is my career and my decision to make."

He crossed to her in an economy of fierce steps and splayed both large hands over her baby mound, his touch far hotter than the winter sun that bore down on them. "These are my children and I'll not allow you to jeopardize their health so you can feed your own ego and continue working."

Heat blazed in her cheeks and burned holes in her indignation. If she thought she was putting her babies in danger, she'd never agree to this. But her doctor had assured her that she was healthy.

And she was bored. So very bored just sitting here day by day.

"You're being unreasonable."

"I am being sane," he said.

No, he was being a bully. "I wouldn't put it past you to post guards to ensure that I don't leave here."

"I would if I thought it necessary."

She stamped a foot, so angry she could scream. "I hate you!"

He had the audacity to smile, a raptor's grin that only spiked her temper. "No, you don't, *querida*. You are angry and behaving petulantly. Once you calm down you will agree that a woman in your delicate condition should not be flying here and there, working long hours."

She curled her fingers into fists so hard her nails bit into her palms. She absolutely abhorred that he expected her to concede defeat, but taking in the rigid set of his broad shoulders clad in a suit jacket clearly tailor-made to his impressive physique, and noting the resolute line of his arrogant jaw, told her that arguing would resolve nothing.

"Our children's safety comes first," he said.

Her shoulders slumped, for while she felt fine and able to work, he was right about one thing. A flight could be very taxing.

He cupped her chin, his touch gentle. "Ring your agent and tell her that you won't be flying to any shoots."

"Fine. You win."

"Good." He dropped a kiss on her mouth, lingering longer than usual, tempting her with how good they'd been in bed, how much she ached for his possession. How she longed to feel desirable in his arms again.

But he'd taken that from them too, and depriving her of that fed her other fear—he no longer found her attractive now she was gaining weight.

He ended the kiss too soon and stepped back, seeming unruffled when her blood was surging with anger and desire.

"I must be going." He lifted his arm to check his wristwatch.

She froze, really looking at her husband this time.

The impeccably tailored suit. The dress shoes. That brusque attitude he wore whenever he was about to embark on a business trip.

"You're leaving," she said, annoyed with herself for being too mad at him to notice what he was wearing earlier.

"I must fly to London today and see to this dispute myself. I shouldn't be gone more than a few days." One shoulder hiked in a careless shrug, a charming gesture she was sure he was unaware he even did. "A week at the most."

He must have reached this decision this morning. It was clear that he'd never intended for her to accompany him, even if it was only to the penthouse in Rio so she would have a change of scenery.

No, he was making it quite clear that her place was here.

"Have a safe trip," she managed to get out, feeling suddenly abandoned.

Again he nodded. "You'll phone your agent?"

Her smile was so tight her face ached, the pain nearly as great as the emptiness yawning in her heart. "Of course."

She pressed the auto dial and seethed with anger that he wasn't going to budge until she caved in to his demand. But when her agent answered with a cheery greeting, she swallowed her anger and got right to the point.

"My husband and I have decided that it's too risky for me to leave Brazil right now and endure a day's session," she said.

"Are you joking?" her agent quipped and not pleasantly.

"I'm serious. My pregnancy is high-risk, and I can't take the chance of flying anywhere," she said.

Rafael bent to place a quick kiss on her forehead before he strode away, clearly smug in the belief that all was well now that she wouldn't leave Brazil.

Her agent muttered something Leila couldn't catch. "You make it sound as if he has you under lock and key."

"That's uncomfortably close to the truth." She was equally sure that he'd instructed his guards to keep her here. "I don't know. Rafael is very overprotective."

"I was thinking more along the lines of overbearing, but it comes out the same," her agent said. "So that's it. You're passing up this gem?"

Leila closed her eyes, thinking about what she was agreeing to, carefully examining the idea that just popped into her head. Dare she?

"No," Leila said at last when the purr of Rafael's car faded in the distance. "There is a way around this."

She bit her lip and stared at her beautiful prison. The one thing that she and Rafael had always guarded closely was their privacy. It was what had allowed them to live in relative peace so many years.

If she acted on the impulse pounding inside her, she would invite the world into their home. She would infuriate Rafael!

But then, she thought with renewed ire, she was just as furious with him for his autocratic ways. He had brought this on himself, she thought.

She was bored out of her mind. Edgy. And growing

more afraid of a relapse as her weight increased and Rafael absented himself from their life.

"Just because I must stay here doesn't mean we can't hold the shoot at my house," she said.

"Hmm, interesting idea. But won't your husband stop you?"

"He just left for London and won't return for days, possibly a week," she said. "How soon can the crew get here?"

"We can move fast. I'll contact them now and call you with their answer."

"I'll be waiting."

CHAPTER TWELVE

RAFAEL stalked from his plane, his mood as gray as the winter clouds scudding over the São Paulo airport. This trip to London had taxed his patience to the extreme.

The glitch in production should have been dealt with swiftly from that end, yet the board had insisted that *he* be there to handle the implementation. After a rough start all had gone smoothly. The new software would be ready for its release date.

Now that problem had been sorted, he could return to Brazil. To Leila and the babies nestled in her womb.

Not a moment went by when he hadn't thought of her. Being away from his wife made him realize how very much he missed her. He'd accused her of believing her career defined her. Laughable in light of this recent business trip. He was just as guilty of the thinking the same thing.

He'd gone from computer whiz kid to techno wizard developer. He had built his company alone, had been in control of it from day one. But it had taken this latest screwup in London and a recanting of his last standoff with Leila to make him realize that it was time to delegate more duties and hand over the reins to someone else.

And at home he had to embrace the role of father.

She'd peeled the skin back and exposed his deepest fears.

Could he trust that she was right? That having one bad parent didn't mean those vile traits would turn up in him.

He was willing to trust her judgment. To open himself up to having a close relationship with his children. To be the parent he'd envied other children having.

But right now the only need pounding in him was for his wife. The urge to hold her, kiss her, make love with her, built inside him as he sped along the rolling highway toward his *fazenda*, toward Leila. Because of her past health issues, and her high-risk pregnancy, he'd held her at arm's length when he longed to do more.

As he'd promised before, there would be no more long separations. He was home to stay for the next few months.

He spared a passing glance at the coffee trees that covered the vast hills. Of the sugarcane fields that came into view.

It was all beautiful. All worth a great deal.

But his family was his most cherished possession.

Family. He still wasn't accustomed to thinking in those terms. To know this time when he returned home she'd be there waiting for him.

The thick gray clouds drifting over his *fazenda* left him more anxious. It wasn't cold, but there was a chill in the air and his concern turned to Leila. Perhaps a few weeks spent in Rio would be welcome right how, for the winters there were much milder than in the Ribeirão Preto highlands.

By the time he sped up the driveway toward his *casa*, he was shaking with the need to find Leila and assure himself she was all right. The last thing he expected to see was a minivan parked in front of the house. He frowned, not recognizing it. A closer look revealed a sticker in the rear window that proclaimed it was a rental vehicle.

He could not guess who was visiting his wife, but a niggling thought in the back of his mind told him he wouldn't like it. Even if this was a welcome guest, their presence annoyed him for he wouldn't be able to have Leila to himself now.

The moment he strode in the door, his gaze sought out the housekeeper. His question to her regarding Leila's whereabouts withered on his tongue as he stared into the salon.

A woman who was a stranger to him was barking out orders like a general to the half dozen people rushing around doing various jobs. Their role instantly became clear.

His salon had been transformed into a set.

He moved forward on stiff legs, anger pulsing through him the closer he got. Auxiliary lights cast a warm glow over a cleared spot in the corner. To the left two plush chairs were angled slightly toward each other. One was empty. Leila sat in the other looking regal but weary.

"Let's try this again and get it right this time," the woman said.

Leila glanced up, her gaze locking on Rafael's. She immediately came to her feet. His tense gaze flicked over the pale blue dress that conformed to her full breasts and well-rounded belly.

The change in her pregnancy was nearly as startling as her defiance. How dare she bring a crew into their home! How dare she tire herself with work!

He set across the salon only to find the way blocked by camera cases and various accessories. "Is this the offer you promised you would refuse?"

"I'll explain later."

Leila moved onto the impromptu set, looking gorgeous and skittish and so damned determined that he knew he was in for a battle with her. A battle he certainly didn't wish to engage in considering her condition and the strangers watching and listening to their every word.

But he couldn't let things ride either. "You went against my wishes."

The color drained from her beautiful face. "Please, Rafael. Not now."

"I'm getting a shadow on the set," the photographer complained, his voice an irritating intrusion.

A touch on Rafael's arm had his dark gaze swinging to the manager who stood at his elbow. "If you'd just step back, sir."

The roar of tense silence finally penetrated his anger. He gave the room a scathing glance, his cheeks heating uncomfortably to realize that all eyes were on him. As if he were the intruder in his own home!

"Of course," he said, moving out of the way when that was the last thing he wanted to do.

One by one the crew returned to their tasks and a low din resumed in the room. His gaze stayed on Leila, but she refused to look at him now.

He willed her to glance his way, and when that failed he willed his thoughts to penetrate her stubborn mind. *Why did you do this? Does your career mean more to you than us? Than our babies?*

"Mr. da Souza, I presume?" asked a woman.

He glanced down at the lady dressed in a tailored suit standing by his elbow. He noted the small writing pad clutched in her hand and swore silently.

"I'm sorry. I don't give impromptu interviews to the paparazzi." Especially those who invaded his privacy!

The woman smiled. "I thoroughly understand. But I'm a staff writer with the magazine, not a roving reporter. Your wife gave us a wonderful interview on her shift in priorities now that she'll be a parent. It's sure to resonate with our readers who are working mothers and must juggle both."

He chose his words with care. "I've no doubt that people are eager to hear her opinion."

"Exactly. Of course she's in a position to set demands— but knowing she places her family first and will only take choice contracts is admirable. She's a role model for many of us," she said. "Anyway, I just wanted to add my congratulations to you on your impending parenthood."

He inclined his head. "Thank you."

Her compliment had the effect of dousing cold water on his raging anger. But his stance hadn't changed regarding his wife working in her present condition.

Down deep he was worried that he and Leila would slip back into the grueling routine that had kept them apart for a year, that they'd slowly drift apart. That he'd lose not only his wife but his children. He couldn't let that happen, which is why he'd insisted she retire.

But looking at her now in their home, poised and gorgeous in her pregnancy, made him realize that he'd destroy what they had if he did force her hand. He'd destroy her if he succeeded in bending her to his will.

It was a chilling realization for him to face.

For the first time in a long time he looked at Leila— really looked at her as a professional. Not his lover. Not his wife. Certainly not the mother of his children.

Yes, she seemed a bit weary. But it was also clear that she was in control, that in her world people rushed to do her bidding—not his. That he was simply the husband of supermodel Leila Santiago.

"Corbin, I need you to loosen up," the photographer said. "You're portraying the adoring father here, so let's get into character. Slide your arms around Leila and rest your hands on her stomach."

A tall lean man he'd not noticed before stepped from the shadows and moved to Leila. He did as the photographer asked but the action looked as strained as Leila's smile.

"You're still too tight," the photographer said. "Leila, maybe if you leaned into him."

She gave a brief nod and stepped back into the man's arms.

"Okay now, relax," the photographer said as he quickly snapped shots, moving to capture different angles. "Bow your head a bit as you come closer to her. A little more. More."

The man was now close enough to kiss her nape, and Rafael stood without breathing, watching. Hating the jealousy that coursed through him like poison.

"That should be it," the photographer said, and the man promptly dropped his hands from Leila and stepped back from her.

Rafael drew air into his starved lungs, calling himself a fool for enduring this particular torture. Though he was well aware she had posed with men many times in her career, often with little clothes on, this stretched his patience to the max.

The whole thing seemed to take an eternity when in fact it was over in a few minutes. But to watch some man lay his damned hands on his wife—on their babies!—was too much for him to tolerate.

He turned to leave, knowing if he stayed he'd likely make a fool of himself.

"Corbin's expression is wrong again and the body language was stilted," the manager said in a clearly perturbed tone that chaffed along Rafael's already frayed nerves. "I'm sorry, Leila, but we'll have to shoot this over."

Rafael turned back in time to see her shoulders droop, to hear her sigh eddy toward him. To feel her frustration reach out to him.

"If she'd relax I wouldn't feel so tense," Corbin said.

How dared this man place the blame on Leila?

"Come on, let's do it again and do it right this time," the photographer said. "We have a plane to catch in two hours."

Rafael took in the set again, jaw clenched so tightly he was sure he'd shatter bone. He was surely better off not being around to watch, and he would have left if he hadn't caught the belligerent glower the male model fixed on Leila.

That snapped the frail thread on his patience. Muttering curses in Portuguese and English, he stormed onto the set.

"What the hell are you doing?" the manager snapped.

"What I should have done earlier." Rafael shot Corbin a look that warned him to back off, which he readily did.

Leila laid a hand on his arm. "Calm down, Rafael."

"I am perfectly calm," he said in a near roar. "They want a picture of you with your husband's hands on your babies, then I will show them how it should be done."

Ignoring the dropped jaws of the manager and photographer, Rafael did what he'd ached to do since he'd walked in the door. He slipped his arms around his beautiful wife and splayed his fingers over her very round belly.

His wife. His children. His life.

In that instant he knew that he could lose all his earthly possessions, his company, his millions. He'd be a rich man as long as he had Leila. As long as he still had her love.

His throat felt thick, his eyes burned. *"Meu amor,"* he murmured as he pulled her flush against his front, groaning as her firm bottom pressed against his groin.

Her light flower scent was divine. She felt like heaven in his arms.

He bent his head and nuzzled her nape, dropping a featherlight kiss on her silken skin. A moan tore from her to mingle with his own husky groan.

She leaned against him, her fingers curling around his wrists in a slow sensual caress that stroked him clear to his soul. He felt the tension escape her and heaved a great shuttering breath as his followed suit.

"That's it," the photographer said. "Keep it up."

But Rafael had no intention of stopping.

This was no act. This was very real.

He'd waited five long days to hold his wife again and he wasn't going to cut this short.

He dropped kisses along the shell-like curve of her ear, the slender column of her neck and then along the gentle slope of her shoulder. He marveled at the change in her body, anxious to see more. To touch, and taste, and lose himself in her.

Dimly he heard the photographer say, "That's a wrap."

Leila turned in his embrace, her face lifted to his. His mouth came down on hers, hungry, demanding.

Her kiss was just as greedy. She threaded her fingers through his hair and held his head still, kissing him in kind. They pulled apart at last, both gasping for breath. Her chin rested on his chest. His forehead was pressed to hers.

The only sound in the room was their mingled breaths and the rapid thud of his heart. A glance at the salon confirmed the others had left. For good, he hoped.

"I am glad that is over," he said after long moments passed and their breathing returned to normal.

She stiffened in his arms, and he knew before he looked down at her face that he'd said the wrong thing to her. "So am I," she said with a good degree of heat. "I am shocked that even you would do something so brazenly arrogant as to storm onto a set and take it over."

It was, by his own admission, beyond bold. But he'd made his point. He'd gotten Leila where he wanted her—in his arms. And he'd gotten the crew out of his house.

But she was clearly not seeing it that way.

She pushed free of him, chest heaving so hard he was sure her ripe breasts would spill from her dress. And just realizing that had him stepping closer, his hands itching to capture them. To help them free of the silky halter constraining them.

To kiss her and hold her and silence this fight before it escalated out of control. "*Querida*, don't you see that I am simply worried about your health and our babies?"

She shook her head, and two fats tears slipped from her eyes. "Yes," she said in a choked voice. "But *I* can't live like a bird in a cage, waiting patiently here for you to set me free for a day. To pay me any attention while you go on with your life."

He drove his fingers through his hair and swore. Of course she was right. She wasn't his trophy to keep hidden away. Today confirmed that more than ever, yet how could he let her return to a career that would take her from him?

He couldn't.

Unbidden came the memory of him when he was very young, of catching a small hare in the alley outside their cottage in Wolfestone. Of him begging his mother to let him keep it.

"I'll take care of it," he'd promised with all the sincerity a boy of eight could manage. "I'll feed it and love it and keep it safe."

"Rafael, what life will it be for the rabbit who has only known freedom?" his mother had asked.

me see a small part of you and it isn't enough. I want you beside me. The man I can discuss my dreams and fears and wants with. My protector. My lover. But most of all, I want you to love me as I love you."

"You think…" But he couldn't finish for she'd already accused him of holding his emotions inside.

She'd admitted she loved him. Admitted that she feared it was one-sided.

How to answer that!

He did hold his thoughts and emotions close, for he had never completely felt certain of their depth before. But now he couldn't continue ignoring the truth.

"Come. I will show you how I feel." He clasped her hand and pulled her down the hall.

"You think sex solves everything?" she cried out, trying to break free, but he merely tightened his hold.

"There is almost nothing I enjoy more than making love with you," he said, "but that isn't my intention right now."

"Wonder of wonders," she said, her tone holding a peevish edge. "You could just tell me how you feel."

He ignored her and walked straight past his office to the next room that she'd assumed was for storage. With a twist of the knob, he pushed the door open and hauled her inside.

"There is a saying my mother favors," he said. "A picture is worth a thousand words."

The retort Leila had been poised to voice withered on her tongue as he pulled her into the large airy room. The light tan walls were covered with framed pictures of her. Magazine covers. Layouts. Stills that she'd forgotten she'd even had taken.

She turned in a circle, certain these depicted the past five years of her marriage and a few before she'd even met Rafael. Yet not one showed them together. Just her.

He'd shrugged, not knowing the answer. Only thinking of what he wanted.

"But I love it," he'd said, near tears for he'd wanted a pet so badly. Wanted a pet to love.

His mother, wise and patient, had merely smiled. "If you love something, set it free. If it doesn't return, it was never meant to be. Remember that in all things, Rafael."

It was a lesson he'd forgotten until now.

Leila was his wife, not his possession. To hold her prisoner here would only make her hate him one day.

"You're right," he said, hiding his frustration and anger and longing behind a bland mask. "I have no right to forbid you to return to work. To force you to stay here. But I won't let us return to the hellish life we led a year ago. My children will know me, Leila. Know us!"

She pressed her palms to her head. "Rafael, I have no intention of working full-time, and I certainly don't want to live apart from you again. I had a fabulous year professionally, but on a personal level it was the worse year of my life. I lost our first child. I was terrified I'd lose you too."

"But you still want to work," he said, still worried that it would consume her again, that what he had in his grasp would slip through his fingers.

"Only when it's a worthy campaign. When it won't interfere with our family." She stepped forward, pressing a hand over his heart that was beating far too fast and too hard. "I want us to escape the pasts that haunt us. Our children deserve a mother who is healthy in mind and body. They deserve a father who is there for them as well. Who'll play with them. Teach them. Who'll love them unconditionally."

"And you think I don't want all of that as well?"

"I thought you did, but of late you've held everything inside," she said, earning a scowl from him. "You only let

SPECIAL EDITION

Life, Love and Family

Karen Templeton

introduces

The FORTUNES *of* TEXAS: Whirlwind Romance

When a tornado destroys Red Rock, Texas, Christina Hastings finds herself trapped in the rubble with telecommunications heir Scott Fortune. He's handsome, smart and everything Christina has learned to guard herself against. As they await rescue, an unlikely attraction forms between the two and Scott soon finds himself wanting to know about this mysterious beauty. But can he catch Christina before she runs away from her true feelings?

FORTUNE'S CINDERELLA

Available December 27th wherever books are sold!

"I loved you from the moment I first met you. But after I lost our first baby, my heart broke knowing I was too afraid to give you want you wanted," she admitted, voicing the truth, making it more painful to bear. "I longed for your child, Rafael, but I feared that if I couldn't give you what you wanted I would lose you and myself."

He bit off an oath in Portuguese. "I am a fool. An idiot who doesn't deserve your love."

"We both lost our way by putting our careers first," she said, voicing the obvious and gaining a grimace from him. "While I don't regret what I've achieved, I, too, have had an epiphany here."

"And what would that be?" he asked, sliding his arms around her, holding her loosely in the circle of his embrace so she could slip free if she wished.

"That in my quiet times I desperately missed you," she said. "That I'd lie awake and wonder if you were thinking of me. That I'd begun to worry that while I was off somewhere alone and exhausted, you'd found someone else to share your life with."

"Never!" he said with enough passion to convince her. "No woman has ever captured my interest but you. I love you, Leila. I've always loved you and always will. But I won't force you to live here—"

Her heart stuttered and she pressed her fingers over his seductive mouth. "Wait! Say that again."

She felt his lips pull into a sexy smile that made her breath catch and her body hum with a different need. "I won't force you to live here because I—"

"No, tell me what's in your heart," she protested, blinking back tears that threatened to fall.

"Because I love you, *meu amor*. Today, tomorrow and forever."

His lips closed over hers, soft, seeking, so tender that the

It was like a shrine. The supermodel. The star shining brightly all alone.

"Why?" she asked, unable to wrap her brain around what this display meant.

"I refurbished this house with great plans to bring you here. To make this our home. But your career took another megaboost that made that impossible." He stared down at their clasped hands, looking far too tense. Too sad. "I have never been as alone as I was then. When a box of your pictures was delivered to the penthouse, I went through them. Just seeing you made me feel alive."

She swallowed hard, unsure if she should be flattered or concerned. She stared at her images on the walls, at Rafael, whose dark eyes glittered with some emotion she'd never seen before but that made her want to go to him, comfort him. Love him. As if she'd ever stopped doing that!

"Oh, Rafael, I wish you would have told me about this house, your plans."

He laughed, the sound having a nervous edge to it. "That would have required me to admit that I was either needy or a romantic fool and my pride wouldn't allow either. So I hung the pictures in my empty house and convinced myself that as long as I could look at your face, I wasn't alone."

"Did it work?" she asked after a long tense pause.

"No, for the longer I stayed here, the more I mourned what we'd lost as a couple," he said. "What I'd lost and feared I'd never regain."

"You never lost me," she said, moving into his arms, cupping his handsome face in her palms. Looking into his intense eyes and finally seeing the little boy who'd stood outside a window in London, looking at the family he'd been denied.

All he'd wanted was a home. A family. Love.

hers for a kiss that left no doubt of the pleasures he vowed to share with her.

Today. Tomorrow. And for the rest of their lives.

* * * * *

tears she tried to hold back broke free. He loved her, and that was all that mattered to her. It had been so long since she'd heard those words. Too long.

"We can live wherever you wish," he said.

"I don't care as long as you're with me."

He gave a shaky nod, his eyes growing suspiciously moist. "As for your career, I promise I won't stand in your way."

She skimmed her fingers over his devastatingly handsome face, over the broad shoulders that had carried the weight of far too much grief in his life.

"I already told my agent that after this next shoot, I won't do anymore until after the babies are born," she said. "And then, I will be very selective about the shoots that I take because my family comes first in my life. I need to focus on these precious babies inside me, Rafael. Our babies. I still worry about relapsing, but I know if you are with me, beside me, I will be stronger. You make me strong, Rafael, and you make me feel beautiful and cherished."

"Good, because I have handed over the day-to-day issues of my business so I can spend more time with you. Together we can do anything, Leila, and I will always be there for you no matter what happens. But I fear I will need your help, too, in being the best father I can be. I need you to show me how to care for our precious babies," he said, his hands sweeping down her back, pulling her closer, fitting her where she belonged—next to his heart.

"Oh, Rafael, you will be an amazing father, and I will help. We will help each other, my love, forever." And she kissed him, showing him by her actions how much she loved him.

Ahh, in this they were always in sync. "So what do you suggest we do with all this free time we'll have?"

"I've an idea or two," he said, his mouth returning to

CLASSIC

Quintessential, modern love stories
that are romance at its finest.

COMING NEXT MONTH from Harlequin Presents® EXTRA
AVAILABLE DECEMBER 6, 2011

**#177 HIS CHRISTMAS
ACQUISITION**
One Christmas Night In...
Cathy Williams

**#178 A CHRISTMAS NIGHT
TO REMEMBER**
One Christmas Night In...
Helen Brooks

**#179 ON THE FIRST NIGHT
OF CHRISTMAS...**
'Tis the Season to be Tempted
Heidi Rice

**#180 THE POWER AND
THE GLORY**
'Tis the Season to be Tempted
Kimberly Lang

COMING NEXT MONTH from Harlequin Presents®
AVAILABLE DECEMBER 27, 2011

**#3035 PASSION AND
THE PRINCE**
Penny Jordan

**#3036 THE GIRL THAT
LOVE FORGOT**
The Notorious Wolfes
Jennie Lucas

**#3037 SURRENDER TO
THE PAST**
Carole Mortimer

**#3038 HIS POOR LITTLE
RICH GIRL**
Melanie Milburne

**#3039 IN BED WITH
A STRANGER**
The Fitzroy Legacy
India Grey

**#3040 SECRETS OF
THE OASIS**
Abby Green

You can find more information on upcoming Harlequin® titles,
free excerpts and more at www.HarlequinInsideRomance.com.

HPCNM1211

"**B**rittany?" His voice was deep and pleasant and made her realize she'd been staring at him openmouthed through the screen door.

"Yes, I'm Brittany and you must be..." Her mind suddenly went blank.

"Alex. Alex Crawford, Chad's friend. You called him about a deck?"

As she unlocked the screen, she realized she wasn't quite ready yet to allow a stranger inside, especially a male stranger.

"Yes, I did. It's nice to meet you, Alex. Let's walk around back and I'll show you what I have in mind," she said. She frowned as she realized there was no car in her driveway. "Did you walk here?" she asked.

His eyes were a warm blue that stood out against his tanned face and was complemented by his slightly shaggy dark hair. "I live three doors up." He pointed up the street to the Walker home that had been on the market for a while.

"How long have you lived there?"

"I moved in about six weeks ago," he replied as they

Harlequin Presents®

USA TODAY **bestselling author**

Penny Jordan

brings you her newest romance

PASSION
AND THE PRINCE

Prince Marco di Lucchesi can't hide his proud
disdain for fiery English rose Lily Wrightington—
or his attraction to her! While touring the palazzos
of northern Italy, the atmosphere heats up…until
shadows from Lily's past come out….

*Can Marco keep his passion under wraps
enough to protect her, or will it unleash itself, too?*

Find out in January 2012!

Harlequin Desire

ALWAYS POWERFUL, PASSIONATE AND PROVOCATIVE.

USA TODAY BESTSELLING AUTHOR

KATHIE DeNOSKY

BRINGS YOU ANOTHER STORY FROM

TEXAS CATTLEMAN'S CLUB: THE SHOWDOWN

Childhood rivals Brad Price and Abigail Langley have found themselves once again in competition, this time for President of the Texas Cattleman's Club. But when Brad's plans are interrupted when his baby niece is suddenly placed under his care, he finds himself asking Abigail for help. As Election Day draws near, will Brad still be going after the Presidency or Abigail's heart?

Find out in:

IN BED WITH THE OPPOSITION

Available December wherever books are sold.

walked around the side of the house.

That explained why she didn't know the Walkers had moved out and Mr. Hard Body had moved in. Six weeks ago she'd still been living at her brother Benjamin's house trying to heal from the trauma she'd lived through.

As they reached the backyard she motioned toward the broken brick patio just outside the back door. "What I'd like is a wooden deck big enough to hold a barbecue pit and an umbrella table and, of course, lots of people."

He nodded and pulled a tape measure from his tool belt. "An outdoor entertainment area," he said.

"Exactly," she replied and watched as he began to walk the site. The last thing Brittany had wanted to think about over the past eight months of her life was men. But looking at Alex Crawford definitely gave her a slight flutter of pure feminine pleasure.

Will Brittany be able to heal in the arms of Alex, her hotter-than-sin handyman...or will a second psychopath silence her forever? Find out in
TOOL BELT DEFENDER
Available January 2012
from Harlequin® Romantic Suspense
wherever books are sold.